Strayed
And Other Stories of
Life on Edge

KT Ashely

Edited by David J. Sebesta
Cover by Zach McCain

KT Ashely is the author of The Pool, a novella

More from KT Ashely
www.authorktashely.com

For Laurie
whose patience and dedication to my success is
ever enduring.

And for Tig and Pop
who most know the road I have traveled.

CONTENTS

SANTA DIDN'T COME

An electronic bleating found its way into my dream world, softly calling me back. Through foggy slit eyes, I could see the early morning Christmas sunrise. Ruffled curtains that were drawn half way open in front of a sliding glass window gave view to dramatic red and orange rays of sunshine that illuminated horizontal clouds. They were shaped like millions of soft cotton balls covering the sky.

The bleating came again. I reached for the night table and grasped the slender black phone in the darkened bedroom.

"Hello," I uttered with the first raspy word of the day.

"Hi Dad! Merry Christmas!" blurted out a young girl's voice.

"Hey Miss Angel Lynn. Merry Christmas, Baby."

I glanced at the clock radio. 6:28 its red numbers shown. *6:28 Central time—as in the morning time*, I considered.

"Did you open your presents?" the voice inquired.

"Not yet, Baby. I have one here from you that I have been waiting to open for when ya'll called. How 'bout you, did you get everything—?"

"Hi Daddy!" a second little voice abruptly interrupted with an ensuing ruckus.

"Kallie Sue?" I asked, but no answer was given.

"That was Kallie Sue; she grabbed the phone away from me and I was talkin' to you." Angel's voice was direct and incensed. Her toddler sister was not well known for her good manners. Being a third grader, my oldest daughter did not have a lot of patience with her sister's antics.

"Alright, ya'll just behave at your Granny's house cause you know how she is."

"Yeah, smoky and grumpy, and I wish I was with you."

The conversation took a quick somber

turn. The children and I had been separated in the divorce a couple of years ago. I was to have them this year for the holidays, but could not afford the plane tickets. It would have taken three days to drive to their Northern New England home from my own beloved Deep South Dixie. Unfortunately, either option would cost dearly in lost wages from work and the exaggerated expense of traveling. All costs for the children to visit me were to be born by me per the divorce decree. My ex-wife had no intention of changing that, and would not agree to split the cost.

"Angel, I love you Babe, and you know that ya'll should be able to come down this summer. We will go fishin' on the bayou and the Zoo and see Paw Paw and Mimi and everybody. This year, ya'll can go crabbin' in this spot I went to a few weeks ago. It will be real fun and it's not that far away—just a few more months."

"Well, how are we gonna get down there cause you couldn't even get us there for Christmas this year and this is the second Christmas we missed with you. Mom is always saying about how you aren't sending all her money to her and—"

"Angel! Angel," I broke in sternly. "Angel, it is Christmas morning and I am sure you called me because you wanted to share your day with me. And that is what I want you to do. Don't worry about what will happen tomorrow. Let's talk about what is happening today. Now, did Kallie Sue get her Sparkle Eyes Barbie I sent her?"

"Yes," said a softening frail voice.

"And what did you get from me?" I asked cheerfully, hoping to pick her spirits back up.

"I got the potter's wheel with clay!" She now was starting to become excited again. "It's great, Dad, and I'm going to make you something today and send it to you."

"That is great, Baby. I tried to get ya'll what you wanted. I'm sorry it's not but just one thing this year."

"That's okay, we really like 'em."

We continued to talk about how the snow there was starting to flurry outside and what their plans were for the day. Angel told me a couple of jokes that I had told as a child myself, although never letting on that I had heard them a million times. I laughed just as hard at them as when she had told the same ones not but a few phone calls ago. She would pause at times and I could sense that she knew I was doing my best not to sound like I was faking happiness. The truth was that we were not exchanging humor, but that the two of us just wanted to hear each other's voice. It is something you do when you can't give the one you love on the phone a hug, because they are two thousand miles away.

"Well, would you see if Kallie Sue will tell me good-bye?"

"Okay, I'll try. Kallie Sue!" Angel screamed across the echoing phone. "Come tell Daddy bye!"

"I don't wanna talk right now," a tiny muted voice was heard to say.

"Did you hear her, Dad?"

"Yeah, I did. She ain' gonna talk till she's ready her own self."

"That's for sure," Angel replied.

"So ya'll have a good Christmas and I'll

call this weekend. And remember, no fighting with Granny or each other."

"Yes, Dad," was replied in an impatient sarcastic sneer.

"I love you and Merry Christmas, Pumpkin."

"I love you too, Dad, Merry Christmas. Bye."

"Bye Sweetheart."

And with that our voices parted and a heavy sadness came over me.

The glowing red sun was now starting to crest between the concealing clouds. It would not be long before the darkness turned to light. And with light came warmth. A gentle breeze was sure to tickle the tinkling wind chimes as they danced. And just under my apartment balcony, the ducks would probe for food in the bayou.

The patch work quilts under which I lay were warm and comfortable. While snuggling there, I began to think of Christmas past and the love felt on this day—a love as inviting as the blankets my grandmother had sewn for me. Looking across the canal, rainbows of color twinkled from rooftops. I wondered if the children across the way had risen to find Santa's treasures.

Sitting up, I drew the remaining curtains from the foot of my bed to espy the holiday vista. But of the half dozen or so homes before me, I saw no lighted windows in the dawn. Surely, there were treasures to be found. Did these children not know what day it was? Or were they like us in our childhood—no need for overhead lights; just dash into the room and be guided by the glow of the blinking tree candles. Yes, certainly that was it! And I myself—had I a visitor last night?

A small, wooden, night table had served as sheltering sentry to an eight inch homemade Tannenbaum. The tree was nobly decorated with red, silver and green sequins. It also had purple, mauve and blue ribbons that were bedazzled with tiny jingle bells. A few golden snowflakes accented the dark green fir needles and a small wooden white dove was perched among the boughs. To crest the beautiful little tree was a simple red and white clinging Kris Kringle. But at her base were only the crumpled wrappings of a small gift that Angel had given me. There were no more.

I had not a stocking to hang as done in years past upon my bed post. And everyone knows that the fat man leaves loads of gifts away from the sleeping ears of children as not to wake them. Perhaps I should wander downstairs just to check and see if I had been a host to someone special last night. And with that thought in mind, I leapt from my cozy covers and into the chilly dawn.

It seemed kind of foolish, a grown man going downstairs to see if an over sized elf had come and left me something. But as I passed the hall night light and turned off its amber glow, the excitement built as steep as the descending stairs. Every step today was pronounced with cushioned carpet between my bare toes. I reached the bottom landing and made a sharp turn onto a cold bare floor in front of the kitchen in my elongated style home. As I peeked in and over the breakfast bar, it all looked the same as I had left it the night before.

Somewhat with empty but hopeful emotions, my legs carried me into the remainder of the large room. Although the light was dim and the air cool, my glance about this place had proven what I as a grown man had already known. Santa didn't come.

But for a few gleeful moments reserved only for children and true believers, a single and lonely father on Christmas day had a spark of hope that could have never turned to reality.

Feeling rather foolish I despairingly returned upstairs, thanked the Lord for my children and asked that the remainder of the day be a happy one for me and others like me.

The next time I awoke, bright rays of warm sunshine had replaced the cool darkness of my room. The central heat had kicked on causing the large plate glass window to partially fog up. It looked like it might rain today I thought. What else was new, it had been raining for a week now.

I was throwing the covers off, when a loud banging and pounding noise crashed up the stairwell. Someone was beating the hell out of my metal trimmed front door.

"Hey! Hold your drawers. I'll be there in a second," I yelled.

Slipping on a pair of oversized sweat pants that had once belonged to my ex-wife, I grabbed a ratty T-shirt and hobbled down the stairs hoping it wasn't female company. There hadn't been time to brush my hair so I did the best I could with my fingers by stroking the unruly nap to make it sit down.

The door stuck a little but came open with a hard jerk.

"Chris, what the hell are you doing on this side of town?"
I asked but had a pretty good idea. His current girlfriend lived only a few buildings away from me.

"I stayed with Patty last night; Sherri was being a bitch," he explained.

"Sherri's always bein' a bitch. Maybe you should just marry her like the rest of us have done and live a normal life."

"Man, if I wanted to hear that crap, I could have stayed at the house last night." Chris was clearly agitated. "But look, you said that you would come by and see me today. I want you to meet my son. All the times that you've come by, you never come in. Let's go to my house and have a drink. It's Christmas and I sure as hell want to enjoy the day."

"Well, let me get it together and we'll take off. I just got up. What time is it? I gotta take a shower, too."

"You need a shower, the way your hair is sticking up like a porcupine's ass." Chris jiggled a bit with his jovial snicker and paunchy belly. "Hey, you got any Myers left?"

"Yeah, you know where to find it. And there's some Coke in there, too. I'll be down in a couple minutes. Turn on some MTV or something. I think they're playing a Liquid TV marathon today. Check it out and see."

Chris and I had met through one of my ex-girlfriend's best friends that he was sleeping with. She and Chris lasted for about three months. My latest girl and I hadn't made it for much longer than they had. It hadn't gone bad for the sex though. Constant and wild was the daily measure. But me being ten years senior to her made this partying twenty-two year old capricious and expensive. Chris had about as good of luck as I did when it came to the ladies. Maybe that is why we hung around as much as we did. But in all the time that I had known him, I never did go inside of his house. I never felt comfortable. Sherri was always there with the kids and Chris seemed so sad when I would drop him off.

Out of the five children living in the home, only one was his. Chris had told me that about six years ago he and Sherri had met at a strip club and then later moved in together. They had a son and Chris accepted the other four children as his own too. The seven of them had lived in the small ramshackle trailer ever since. It was only a few months ago that Chris had decided that this was not the life he wanted. He had gotten a fair paying job with a cement company as a laborer, but during this rainy season things slowed down. Sherri became the welfare type, and didn't have much ambition other than for dancing. But with age and kids the clubs she could get work at just got sleazier and less profitable for her.

As the clean, clear hot water cascaded over my soapy body, I thought of my friend and his family. Had Santa come to their home? What had the children to open this year? I was lucky that I had a steady job at the restaurant. Line cooks didn't make a whole lot of cash, but at least I worked every week. And there was always something to nibble on when I was hungry.

"Hey Chris, did you find what you needed down there?" I asked stepping from the bathroom.

"Yeah, man. Hey, where did you get these tamales? These are serious!"

"A guy at work brought them to my boss. He gave me a dozen of 'em. They're the best I've ever had." I grabbed a shirt that looked free of wrinkles and slipped on a pair of scuffed brown cowboy boots. "There is some smoked salmon down there, too. One of my father's clients gave it to him, but they don't like it so they gave it to me. Did you see it?"

"What the hell is *smoke sallon*?"

"Salmon. It's a fish that rich people eat. Sometimes they smoke it and jack the price up. It's pretty good though." At this point I had made my way down and was standing in the kitchen with my friend as I finished buttoning up the remainder of my shirt.

"The only smoked fish I've ever eaten was mullet that came out of the bayous linked up with Lake Pontchartrain. Between the polluted lake and the natural smell of the fish, you gotta smoke it to eat it."

We both chuckled a bit and Chris finished his second rum and coke with a big swig before we made our way out. I slammed the front door behind us and made tracks for the truck.

"You want to stop off at JP's and get some beer?" Chris asked.

"Sure man, I got a couple of bucks." It was the least I could do; I figured his cash was running pretty low. The rain had seen to that.

It hadn't taken long after our stop at the convenience store to get across town to the backwoods community where Chris lived. I myself had lived here once. The first place I rented after the divorce was in this neighborhood, that after moving from my parent's home. My old trailer was a few streets down from his. Most of the folks living in this area were poor. It had its share of white trash, too. As a matter of fact, white was the only thing in this neighborhood. No black person would dare step back here. I had moved here because of the cheap rent. It was a contrast to the way I had been brought up. On the walls of my childhood home were hung abstractions of Georgia O'Keeffe. Most of these people's homes were decorated inside and out with the same type of cheap fake flowers she painted pictures of during her New Mexico Era.

We pulled into the make shift muddy drive bouncing over the exposed roots of a grand, old, Southern Oak tree. Two black and tan mixed breed dogs emerged curious from underneath the raised trailer. The younger one set both legs in front of himself as to crawl and with hind-end in air, stretched and yawned as if he were a Van Winkle descendant. The old bitch, which I presumed to be the mother, approached me slowly with tail wagging and grotesquely sagging teats swaying in unison.

"I didn't know you hunted coon," I said inquisitively to Chris.

"I don't. Them damn dogs would'n know a coon from a polecat," Chris jested. "Ain't worth a damn. One the kids brought that Mama dog home a couple years ago as a puppy from the neighbors down the road and I've been throwing her youngins in the river ever since. I missed that little bastard there one morning and the kids took and hid it till Sherri made me promise to let 'em keep it."

"Hell Chris, you know how kids are—they need something to call their own." He shrugged his broad shoulders at my comment.

As the two of us balanced our way up the path made from scrap lumber laid over the soggy ground, I noticed a half hidden face glancing from behind a broken window. The jagged pane had been covered with an upside down, dirty and faded burlap feed sack that partially read:

FER Y MORS
COW PEA   HULLED
N W ORLEANS

The rest of the thirty-plus year old single wide trailer was not in much better shape over all. What must have been white now was covered in a green shade of algae moss. An unfinished deck, made of unsecured plywood and two-by-fours, was leveled at the bottom of the door frame. It was a good four and a half feet high from the ground. There were no rails, so God help anyone that fell or slipped through the planks as they were sure to land on one of a number of pieces of junk which littered the yard.

"Come on in," my host greeted as he wrenched open a heavy, rickety and wooden homemade door.

I began to follow in apprehension as to what I might find around the corner. But before I stepped in, my foot first scooted the dog's slop pot out of the way. The movement stirred up the foul stench of rotten, sloshy, grey mush. Peering in I could see the interior of the home was dark, dirty and unkempt. It smelled profusely of unemptied ashtrays and stale liquor. Piles of stray clothes were scattered over the outlines of furniture. When I attempted to shut the bulky door behind me, it screeched across the torn linoleum floor as I heaved.

"Lift up on it," Chris commanded.

I did as instructed and the entrance was

secured. The fresh, cool air was shut out. Then there came into the mix a familiar smell of stewing beans and also that of marijuana. But both were undermined with another sweet odor—a petroleum one. I soon noticed from whence it came.

The red glow of a kerosene space-heater lit up a cluttered corner of the kitchen. It seemed a foolish place for an open flame because a propane gas fed hot water tank sat idly behind it in a doorless cabinet. And to the right—two plastic milk jugs with amber liquid I could not identify from the distance.

"Stop throwing that goddamned basketball in the kitchen! An' stop that runnin' right now; damn you little piss ass, TJ and Erica!" a very animated, overall thin, and rusty, short haired woman shouted. She had a cigarette dangling from her pout lips with squinted eyes from the tobacco smoke. The man's ribbed undershirt she wore loosely draped her once firm full breasts. It was a dirty off-white and stained but still thin enough to expose her rather large pink areola yet small bud nipples. The bottom of it was tucked over a small, round, belly with love handles into a size-too-small pair of hot pink, cotton, booty shorts. The tight fit gave her a prominent camel-toe front, and a shapely ass; it left little to my imagination when she bent over to pick up a clove of garlic that had fallen on the floor.

But the woman's shrill warning was not heeded in time and the faded orange ball banked off of the heater causing a large flaring flame to hiss loudly. It had dunked tightly against the water tank's tarnished flexed tubing where it remained—a catalyst for someone to get a sure whooping.

"Hey Sherri," I called.

"Hey Man. You and Chris been 'hoin' again?" she asked snidely as she stood back up and kicked another piece of trash from under her bare feet.

"I ain't been 'hoin'—I stayed with him last night," Chris quickly butted in.

"Now Sherri, you know I don't 'ho around—and your 'ol man was with me."

Stepping closer to her, it was obvious the world had not been kind to this once stunning beauty. Now in her late twenties, life projected a woman of twice her age. I leaned to her ear as to kiss her and whispered conspicuously, "Besides, I'm waiting for you to run off with me." This playful lie was given to offset the first—but she already knew Chris wasn't with me the evening before.

She turned her back to me and bumped me firmly toward the living room area with her scantly clad bottom and said, "You just want that ass. Go sit the *Fuck* down with your other bitch."

Faking rejection, I made my way around the breakfast bar navigating the littered path into the next room.

"Do I know you?" a little voice rudely inquired with mischief in his voice.

"Do I know you?" I asked back sharply.

"This is my son, TJ," Chris said.

"I'm four," the child commanded, holding up five, grungy, little crooked fingers.

"That's five fingers, Dodo," Sherri corrected from the kitchen that I had just left.

It was becoming obvious that manners were not the major concern in this household. It seemed that the children, or at least the two that

I had met, were products of their parent's own inequities. They appeared rude, rambunctious and without reverence for anyone—all characteristics of both Chris and Sherri. I sometimes wondered why I was friends with this man. Or was it more that I was a friend of his making?

As I found my way to a sticky green vinyl couch with what appeared to be cigarette burns in the arm rests, a dirty blonde headed little girl about the same size as TJ, jumped in the spot I was about to sit down in.

"Hey girl," I exclaimed.

"Don't sit on me," the pitched giggly voice said.

"Then you better move over." I recalled that my own daughters loved to play this game. Just before you sit down, the child would jump into your seat. If they were lucky enough to find the sitter in a good mood, a playful and gentle squash would be the reward.

"You know what?" my new seating partner questioned as she now was beginning to boldly crawl into my lap. "Santa Claus forgot to come to my house last night."

"That's 'cause ya'll were all ugly this year," Sherri yelled from the kitchen while tossing herbs into the boiling soup pot.

I was beginning to dislike this home even more. Maybe I was right not to have come in on previous invitation.

"Well, Santa didn't come to my house either," I consoled.

"TJ and Erica, go play," Chris yelled.

The two children immediately scampered off to a darkened back room as if they knew the procedure.

"Where's the rest of the kids, Sherri?" I inquired to make conversation.

"They went to my sister's house for the day. She didn't want the babies, so they stayed with me."

"Sherri, you gettin' that rum down?" Chris asked impatiently.

"Yeah, hold your ass. I gotta stir these beans and rinse some glasses."

It wasn't long before my hosts had set an almost full bottle of store brand rum on the coffee table in front of us. There was a two liter cola bottle of some brand I had not heard of before and cubed surplus cheese atop crackers which tasted as if they had been bought at the day old store. It was thoughtfully arranged on a paper plate. The TV was turned up loud with a Three Stooges marathon. Sherri was sitting in Chris' lap, his hand between her slightly parted legs. My lap was the recipient of two blackened bare feet that led up to long, silky smooth and sun freckled legs, ending in a pair of hot pink, pantyless, shorts that now were being breached by my male host's fingers. I began to drift off into my own world as they had done in theirs.

Christmases past had been much happier for me before the divorce. The girls and I would snuggle up in a chair on the cool morning and watch the video tape of Rudolf. My wife would heat hot chocolate and ask who wanted marshmallows. I hated the confections. The children loved them. We would have a nice lunch with all the trimmings of a New England tradition. Afterwards, we would exchange phone greetings with our friends and neighbors. Every year it was pretty much the same, a warm and loving Christmas family.

Stampeding feet broke me from my

daydream.

"I'm gonna get that ball first," TJ hollered.

"I want it first," his sister yelled.

The two children ran into the kitchen breaking the hour or so of varying silence. Neither could remember where the object was, and I knew that when they found it, a donnybrook was sure to ensue.

"I got it!" TJ exclaimed as he leapt between the kerosene heater and the hot water tank.

The young boy grasped the ball with excitement, snapping the tarnished old gas flex pipe. Not comprehending the smell of the spewing gas, but as any youngster would do in reaction to breaking something, he quickly retreated backward knocking over the open flame heater.

TJ was able to exit a few steps to the back of the trailer from the kitchen when a large expulsion of hot flame and liquid kerosene which had been stowed in the milk jugs splashed toward us. Sherri grabbed little Erica as Chris and I struggled to gain footing.

Fuel and flames spat at us in a large red and orange fireball reminiscent of the earlier morning's sunrise. He jerked the clumsy door open as flames from some of the spill lapped at his waist.

Sherri and the baby ran out first; Chris was behind them. I had fallen to the floor and thought to get to TJ but the entire kitchen was engulfed in hot orange flames and black smoke that seemed to be raining from the ceiling. There was nothing I could do for the child and regretfully decided to follow Chris.

As I was stumbling out of the door, I could see my friend falling over the side of the unfinished deck. A second explosion inside had splashed burning liquid onto the back of my friend in his escape. The flames on his burning pants and shirt nipped at his hair. Sherri was screaming as she ran to him, setting the girl baby aside.

"Chris, Chris!" she shouted as she tried to extinguish the flames with bare hands.

I made my way down the steps to give aid. Chris had landed onto a rusted motorcycle engine in the fall. The ground was soaked with rain and Sherri was now trying to roll him in the mud. There was a light sheet of cold drizzle falling from the sky. Erica was too much in shock to cry and though tears streamed down her tiny face in the rain, the only noise to come from her mouth was that which sounded like she had the hick ups—her little body jilting as she convulsed.

"Chris—are you OK, man?" I questioned. But as I asked I could see through a burned pant leg that burns were not his only problem. A jagged red bone had poked through the skin just above his ankle.

"Sherri, get the baby and go call 911," I commanded. She was frozen with fear.

Another frail but agonized little voice screeched from the interior of the trailer.

"TJ! TJ!" Sherri screamed his name as if a hot steel rod had been run through her torso. Her cry shot up through the nerves of my spine.

"Call the goddamned fire department now!" I instructed again. "I'll get TJ." But she fell on her knees clutching Erica's tiny hands. It was just as well, as a small crowd of neighbors now began to rush to the scene.

I began to run to the back of the trailer, but tripped over the old bitch as I was rounding the corner. I didn't know who was more confused, the dog or myself in all that had happened.

After pulling my knee out of the mud, I continued, dodging junk piles with every few strides. As any father would I could hear the frail sobbing of the young child inside the burning pit knowing that if I could hear his screams from the outside, he must be in terror—but alive.

The back of the trailer looked much like the front, algae moss covering the once white sheeting. From what I believed to be another entrance, thick black smoke poured from the top doorway. It was cloaked with a ratty old red and black flannel blanket that had been soaked by the rain. I grabbed the cloth and tore it from its nailed appendages. Hot air and gases immediately spewed out like a dragon's breath. I could see no child.

"Jesus, you have taken my children— please let this one live to know his father!" I desperately prayed aloud. And with that and the memory of my own children on my mind, I wrapped the red wet blanket around my body and dodged into the burning compartment.

"TJ! TJ—where are you, son?"

The room was hot and the smoke thick and choking. My eyes watered and stung with chemical burn. I did not know that a building could go up so fast. The air was black and it caused me to crawl on the cluttered floor. It was so dark that all I could do was hope that the child had hid in a safe place. I bumped into what I thought were walls until I could go no farther. But from behind the wall I now faced, I heard sobbing muted by the roar of the blaze in front of me. The way was narrow, so it could only have been a door. I reached for the knob, but it had been locked from the inside.

"TJ. Open the door, TJ." But no response was given. Only the muffled crying persisted.

I knew the frightened child could not respond. The fire was beginning to creep over head as bits of the hot and melting plastic ceiling began to drip down onto me, sizzling on the wet blanket. I stood up and burst through the door with my shoulder as a battering ram.

Falling at the child's feet, I gagged and coughed hoarsely deep from within my lungs after smashing the side of my face on the toilet. I rose to my knees and still coughing and clutching the red blanket around my body, looked into the child's scorched and blackened face, only to hear with tearing eyes a frail voice say: "Santa—you came."

I did not know what to make of it other than the ramblings of a confused and traumatized child. I scooped up the young boy. We navigated with hands on wall corners until we crawled earnestly out of the fire through the back entrance whence I came. A tall man in a fireman's suit grabbed for us at the doorway exit as we rolled out to descending grey light. He snatched the boy from me as I fell to the ground. Another man pulled me to my feet from the freezing muddy ground. The cold drizzle was beginning to increase now and the spray from the volunteer department's fire hoses added to the muck puddles.

Sherri grabbed at TJ in the fireman's arms as I rounded the back of the trailer and I could see them tending to Chris' leg near a water truck. The crowd had grown a bit and it looked as if people were waiting to catch the next ride at a carnival. I never did like the idea of coming to see someone else's tragedy. But people have a morbid side. What did they expect to see? No one died here today. Only a family has lost everything that they had, what little it was.

As I made my way to the sides of Chris and Sherri, I took Erica by the hand and lifted her to my hip and hugged her. It had been some time since I had held a little girl. We were given dryer blankets to cover up in, and I thanked God that my own children were safe and warm at home.

"Hey man, you got my son outta there," Chris said to me with tears in his eyes and a cracking voice. "Man, I can't tell you—"

"Hey...I have kids, too," I interrupted. "Nothing needs to be said. Just love your babies, and your ol' lady."

Chris took Sherri's hand and squeezed it tight.

"I do love you, Sherri," he told her.

"Then stay home with me and the kids

and stop whoring all the time," she begged.

"I think this man just showed me how much I love you and TJ and the rest of the kids. I want a better life. Maybe we will get a chance to start over again now," he told her.

Sherri just nodded. The mechanical pitch of whining water pumps behind them kept the fire dowsed as tears flowed down her cheeks.

"That's the man who saved my boy's life. That's the man, TJ," Chris stated.

TJ looked up at his mother's drawn and weary face from where she held him close underneath the warming blanket.

"Santa came, Mama. Santa didn't forget my name. Santa came and got me," the little boy said.

I looked at the child in his mother's arms as I held his clinging sister. His face was black and his hair was burned close to his head. He had no eyebrows and I could see the skin starting to blister on his cheeks and neck. This poor child had just lost everything, but then nothing material did he have to lose. All he wanted was to be remembered by Santa. It is all that perhaps anyone wanted. I don't even know if my friend remembered my name at present. But TJ and I do know this—Santa did. And he came after all.

"Hey," a man with pen and notepad shouted at me with query in his eye, "did they say you pulled that kid from the fire?"

"Maybe they did," I replied reluctantly.

"What's your name—I'm from the City Post."

"My name?" I paused. "Just put Santa," I muttered. "No one will remember it past tomorrow."

THANK YOU FOR YOUR SERVICE

The register sputtered loudly with a quick and repetitive *clack-   clack-clack-clack-clack— Clank.* The repetitive clatter stopped abruptly as the cash drawer bolted open and concluded with a *swoosh* of loose coins from the day's collections.

"A dolla'-thirty-seven today, Mr. Bob".

The late sixty something and balding plump man averted his eyes from the wall photo of a nuclear submarine and then back to the baker at the counter.

"I don't know why anybody would want to get on a perfectly good ship that sinks. You musta had a death wish son," the patron expressed.

"Well no, sir, just a little crazy I suspect—full of piss and vinegar in those days," said the cashier as he smiled wide and handed the loyal customer back sixty-five cents in change. The purchaser's hand was large, soft and accommodating but did not dwarf the bulky Knights of Columbus ring he wore.

"You know, I almost got drafted for Viet Nam. Joined the Guard and was lucky enough to stay state side. Did my full two years near Biloxi." He stuffed half of the klobasnek into his mouth. The sausage and cheese Czech pastry was often marked down at the end of the day. The gentleman knew this on his way home from work at the city code office. He was a regular almost every other day around five-forty-five, just when the bakery also was giving out free coffee if there was any leftover.

"Guess you just lucked out, Mr. Bob."

The door cracked open with a tinkle from a brass bell bouncing off of its glass front pane. With an unseasonably cold and brisk rush of November air, a strong whiff of urine and harsh body odor also whisked in.

The hefty man glanced indignantly toward the offending smell as he finished filling his paper cup with the fragrant dark roasted brew.

"Yeah, I did in a way, but I also helped keep the home front secure. Even though in those days we weren't considered part of the military. You know, I don't even get VA benefits?"

"I had no idea," remarked the attendant as he waved *hey* to a hobbling stiff legged man. He wore a thin, dirty red windbreaker.

"Yep, and some of these bums I grew up with around here didn't even do a damn thing." He threw his wooden stir stick into the small chromed dispenser. A second staunch eye contact with the baker emphasized his insinuated disgust with the newly arrived client."

"Well, I know you did good by serving our country, young man. Thank you for your service. I'll see ya'll next Monday. Hope dem Saints put tha' whoop ass on Atlanta this weekend," he called out as he pulled the tinkling door back open and let in another *whoosh* of frigid air.

"Yep, see you next Monday, Mr. Bob. Least the Saints are playin' in the Dome this

Sunday." They waved silently to each other as the door closed between their salutations.

Two men both veterans of their own wars were left alone in the closing bakery as the sunlight quickly turned to dark. One had served in a cold war under black water as brisk as the outside night. The other had fought in the jungles of the fore-mentioned country noted by the rapacious man.

"Mr. D, you really need to get to the shelter tonight."

"Aww, um-K," the vet slurred, expelling a heavy breath of nondescript alcohol. "I feel pretty warm right now. An' I got dat Indian blood."

"Yes sir, I know but last time you also had frost on your ass you told me. You still got that sleeping bag we got the other day?"

The man straightened up as best he could on his cloaked disfigured limbs and ran his grime soiled hands through his matted black hair. After a moment of swaying pause he replied, "Yes, sir. And I love Jesus."

"That's good. I know you do."

The baker put several day old meat

pastries that he had held back earlier, two baking apples and a can of Barq's soda plus a bottle of water in large paper bag. As he handed the package to the tattered man, they embraced with a firm full bodied hug.

"I'm the strongest Coonass Injun in d's parts," he declared as the bear hug lifted the proprietor's feet off the ground.

"Yes sir, you are, Mr. D."

He put the man down gently. "I love you, Brother."

"I love you, my friend. Make sure you come back by here tomorrow."

The pastry maker stood in front of a large icy glass window as the aging soldier hobbled across the narrow street. The man navigated his well known path through the pot holed parking lot of an abandoned warehouse as if he were on patrol. Silently the chef watched in sentry fashion, remembering the man's haunting stories until he no longer could see his friend's silhouette. It had faded around the dark corner of the grey derelict building.

The baker turned off the OPEN sign and locked the door for the evening. On the counter top from where the old veteran had been standing, the chef picked up three small tarnished coins that the man had left as payment for his supper. With a rattle and a clunk, they were placed in the register below the ship's photograph on the wall.

END OF THE LINE

Blood streamed over Alan's wrist into a furious whirlpool of draining water. His reflection in the bathroom mirror was obscured by a damp mist.

"Come on damn it—stop bleeding," Alan shouted as he pressed the soft gauze into his sliced flesh. His training as a Navy Hospital Corpsman had come instinctively back to him. He could feel his veins swell as the compress bore into the wound.

The cut throbbed. His heart pumped. There was numbness about him—a void. In the mist, his senses drifted and his ears rang.

"Jeez, that was stupid. I could have killed myself."

He pushed a bottle of peroxide aside with his elbow and tore the securing surgical tape to his dressing with his teeth. Before hopping onto the vanity counter, Alan wiped it dry with a blood-splattered white terry towel. He went over it twice as the first run left pink streaks on the cold marble surface. The cloth was replaced neatly on the edge of the sink.

"Crisis center," he mumbled. "She's even got a sticker with the number on the side."

With twitching fingers, he punched the numbers on the cordless phone. From his outer shirt pocket Alan pulled out a half pack of Camel "straights" and a silver souvenir lighter that read: USS Guam LPH 9. The phone exchange began to ring as Alan sparked the flint. The lit wick gave off a sweet waxy smell.

"County Crisis Line, this is Rita, how can I help?"

The quick answer to his call caught him by surprise, and the first long drag of his cigarette was coughed back into the receiver.

"Jesus, I'm sorry," he said with a strained voice and watering eyes. "I need some help."

"What's the problem?"

"What?" he asked.

"What is the problem—are you okay?"

the young voice asked.

For a moment, the voice at the end of the line haunted him. It was familiar; maybe not so much the tone but the words spoken.

"Yeah, I'm alright. But you gotta speak up a little more—my ears are still ringin'."

"Did you take any drugs? Any pills?"

"No, no--nothing like that. I'm not trying to kill myself. There was just this loud noise. It'll clear up soon."

"Well, what is your name and what can I do for you?"

"Alan. I'm feeling a bit depressed. Things are really screwed up and I really need somebody to talk to before I lose it."

"What is it that's screwed up?"

"Well…this divorce thing has gotten me a bit worked up lately. I've been thinking things I shouldn't be." Alan fidgeted with a mother of pearl inlaid silver band on his right ring finger.

"A lot of people get divorced. It's okay to express anger. Try to get it out so it doesn't build up. Are you divorced now?"

"Yes, and I have been for a few years. The woman left me and my girls. It was just a couple days before Valentine's. We were married for seven years. Guess she got the itch." Alan gently rolled a gray-black ash into a carnival glass ashtray before inhaling deeply once again. His pulse was beginning to slow.

"I'm sorry. That was pretty cold hearted. She could have waited a few days."

"She waits for no one. She takes what she wants, and destroys the rest. Just like Sherman through Atlanta."

"You mean she's a northern girl?"

"No. She's from a small town in South Carolina. We met when I was stationed there in the Navy—though I think her people were Carpetbaggers."

"Aaah, a sailor are you?" the familiar voice returned.

Those words had been spoken years before. It was in a little bar called "The Chicken Drop". The club had earned its name by a game of chicken roulette of sorts. Patrons bet a minimum of five dollars on numbers ranging from one to thirty-six. When all bets had been made, a chicken was released into a pen that had numbered squares on its floor. Whatever number the chicken happened to crap on, that was the winning ticket. Sailors came for the gamble. Women came for the sailors—and their cash.

"That was years ago," Alan said. "And I wish I had never set foot in that port."

"But don't you have some good memories? What about your daughters? Surely if you hadn't been there, you would have never had your girls," she said. "Maybe that's the best part from your marriage."

The conversation stopped and a brief silence ensued. Alan thought back to when he and children would wrestle and laugh loudly on the living room floor. He would pick a girl up while lying on his back and shake each youngster in the air. The child would squeal with delight. Then she would reach for her mother's leg playfully. The woman ignored her and would get up to turn the TV's volume louder. When she returned, she pushed her chair out of reach from the jovial playmates. Their mother then replaced her own thumb that she had been sucking on, back in her mouth. It had been a scene repeated many times in the home over the years. His wife didn't seem to want affection from any of them.

"I suppose my girls were the best part of my marriage," Alan said.

"Hey. I know it must be tough. I'm sure you are a very nice gentleman. You express your love for your girls so deeply. Any normal woman would be lucky to have you. You said you've been divorced for, what--three years? Don't you have a girlfriend?"

"I did. But she turned out to be like the rest of 'em." Alan looked down at the mother of pearl ring he wore as he habitually turned it with his thumb. "All she left me with was a trinket. And the memory of her sleepin' with another man."

"Oh. I'm sorry. But hey! You still have your girls with you, right?"

"No" Alan snapped. "The judge gave them back to her for no good damned reason. It's a crock of crap. Nobody gives a damn. I had a vasectomy after my youngest was born. My ex-girlfriend left me cause I couldn't give her a kid and now she's pregnant with another jerk's baby an' she an' my ex-wife have what I should—kids! It's wrong."

The mist on the mirror was beginning to fade. Alan could see the outline of his face and chest as he turned to the basin to wet his brow. Hopping from the counter, a piece of shattered tile crackled under his feet. He stooped down to pick it up. From the corner of his eye, a lifeless outline lay crumpled in the tub. There was a tinkling sound that came from its open drain, much like that of pouring a thin stream of thick motor oil into a hollow pipe.

Rita became uncomfortable from hearing his sudden outburst. She did not know what to say. It was only her second week as a Crisis Line volunteer. In all twenty of her short lived years, she had never heard of such a tragic family story. Her parents had been lovingly married for over twenty-five years. Her emotions swelled inside of her.

"No man deserves to be treated like that," she blurted.

"Well, deserve it or not, women do it to us everyday."

"Not all women are like that, Alan. I would never treat anyone that way. If I had a boyfriend who loved me, he would be the center of my life. I know what it means to be lonely—to be abused by others. I've had my share of jerks too."

"I guess everyone has--some more than others."

"Alan, you need a good friend. Someone who can be there for you."

"Right, Rita. Who's that? You—the girl on the end of the line?"

"Why not? Are you gonna go around mad at the world?"

"I didn't say I was. I just don't trust much anymore."

"I'd never hurt you."

A sharp pain ran up Alan's arm and it seemed to leap to his forehead. He had heard the girl's voice, but there was something familiar in the words. "Why should I believe that?" he asked.

"I have nothing to hide. I have no motive to gain. I just think you are interesting." Rita felt more pity than true interest. She thought, *if only I can get him to realize that someone can love him.*

Alan stared at the slick vinyl floor below him. Upon the white tile, an empty red 12 gauge shotgun shell lay motionless. His cold eyes peered through it. The black OO marking seemed to stare back at him. A trance like state had momentarily enveloped his mind.

"Good things can come out of bad," she said. "I believe there is a purpose for everything."

"You're right. After all I did call and got a hold of you. You seem to really care. You haven't cut me down. You say you understand, and you have a nice voice too."

"Thank you. You seem to be a sweet man. I only wish you weren't so sad."

"I'm sure I'll be OK."

"You know, Alan, like I said, if you find yourself a good friend—things will turn around for you. Don't be scared to take a chance. You never know who you will meet."

"Who is gonna want a man like me. I can't have kids, I'm depressed about my daughters, and my ex-wife constantly is harassing me. No woman is gonna want to put up with that."

"But it's your good qualities we look for. You are caring, responsible, you sound well educated and must have a good job. How 'bout your looks—I bet you're tall and quite handsome. I can tell by your voice."

"I'm about six foot."

"And single too," she added.

"Didn't you say you don't have a boyfriend?"

"Yeah, I'm afraid that's true. Just haven't found one nice enough lately," she stated.

"Well, do you think I might be able to meet ya sometime?"

Rita's radiant self-assuredness dropped. She had been so wrapped up in trying to save this man that she did not see her own egotistical set-up coming. The rule was, never get personally involved.

"Alan, I don't...*Alaan... Alaan... Al*...aan."

"Alan. Wake up," a familiar voice echoed. "Alan."

His head was foggy and his mouth was dry. The room seemed to spin and for a moment he felt the bed sway as if he were on the ship.

"Fuck! I missed movement." He grabbed for a phantom privacy curtain.

"Alan! You're at home. Wake up, Honey. You're in The Pass. Pass Christian. It's me!" A tender soft hand squeezed his shoulder from behind. Out of the corner of his eye he could make out the shadowed silhouette of bare breasts and dangling light hair enrobing them.

"HuuuuuuggH," he gasped. "Stacy...Stace."

"It's me...I'm here Babe".

"Jesus. I had that dream again. And I thought I was on the boat."

"You are home." She kissed his cheek and held her bare body close to his own naked back. "You have an appointment with the Doc today. And group. It's gonna be alright. Shhhh."

It wasn't far to the Biloxi VA. Alan took the coast road in. The drive along the water relaxed him. White sand glittered in the sun and people were beachcombing for shells and sand dollars in the midmorning light. The air was clean and salty. The sun was warming and bright. He felt his spirits lift as he navigated through the narrow gates of the facility. Even the somber marble head stones in the cemetery seemed to exude comfort as he passed by them.

Alan found a perfect parking spot under a weathered Live Oak tree that had survived Katrina. The hospital reminded him of port calls in the Mediterranean—the architecture anyway. Breezy white and cream buildings with red brick colored roofs bestowed a memorable motif.

The Gulf Coast VA's interior was newly renovated. Its open spaces were much more inviting than most other government infirmaries. Some of the VA Centers, like Atlanta, were old and crowded. And they were often staffed with civilian "government welfare" employees who did not give a damn about anything more than their own benefit packages. All they need do is show up for work to get it. *To Hell* with the reason they were hired and those that kept them in a job. But the staff here was friendly and welcoming. They truly seemed to care for the most part.

"Name and last four?" a young woman with smooth coffee toned skin and attractive natural hair questioned as Alan arrived at the reception cubicle.

Alan gave her the information she asked for along with his stylized patriotic picture ID card. He stood quietly as she typed in his confirmation. Her tight curls cascaded to her shoulders and he thought to himself—'why do the Sisters straighten that beautiful hair'? He had grown up in the 70's and loved the days of sexy sista's like Pam Greer and Chaka Khan. Some white girls tried to capture the look in the 80's, but they didn't have anything on those gorgeous girls.

It wasn't long before Alan was called back and seated in his therapist's office.

"So Alan, what's going on today?" a younger man with a slight Hispanic accent asked. The man was of medium build, tan browned skin and wore a shirt that fit his toned body in a fine tailored fashion. The clinician looked to be in his late thirties. He sported slick short-cropped hair, contemporary eye glasses and had a calm voice. The faint smell of rose water was about him. No doubt, he was eye candy for the ladies in reception. On an earlier meeting, he had told Alan that he too was a Navy Veteran.

"Doc, I've been having dreams of killing my ex-wife again. They are kinda crazy and my wrists are cut, too. Sometimes. But they sometimes aren't. They just heal up or something."

"Have you been thinking of suicide again, Alan?"

"No. Just the dreams. And when my wife woke me up this morning, I thought I was on the ship."

"What meds are you on, Alan?"

"No meds, Doc. I don't want anything. Years ago I was. My daughter was beaten up by her step-dad and then they institutionalized her for a while. I had a little breakdown from that. Lost my little business, too. They put me on Prozac but it made me fat and foggy. Kinda like Santa—jolly and roly. And it made my head kinda weird. I don't like not being in control. And at my age I don't need the added weight gain either."

"Well, is anything going on? Any new stress at home?"

"Things are OK with Stace and me. At the moment."

"This is your second wife?"

"No. My third," Alan replied softly.

"Sooo. Which wife is it in your dreams? asked the therapist as he scrolled through the patient's file at his computer.

"It's my first. I think. The mother of my children. She lives in New Hampshire. So do my girls."

A pause lingered as the clinician scanned for query within the notes before he responded. "Is this dream the same one mentioned in the past few sessions? I mean, is it always the same scenario?"

"Yeah, I think so," Alan said. "Pretty much I go into the bathroom at our old house and shoot the bitch in the head with a shotgun. But I don't ever see her face. Just a slumped body in the tub."

"You don't see her face," the therapist stated. "So how do you know who it is?"

"I just feel like that's who it is. But I

have been concerned a bit that it might be someone else."

"Like who, Alan?'

"Well, it's a dream, so funky stuff happens. I think last night I was talking to a girl at a crisis center after I shot her. But like I said, I didn't see her face. Her face is always turned away."

"Do you think it might be your wife—your current wife? Stacy?" the man asked.

"No, I don't think so. Remember I told you that my first wife left my children and me when we lived in Nashua. We went back up there after the Navy to be close to her family. Eleven years later I woke up one morning and she said she didn't want to be married anymore. I thought I'd never see my kids again, but she said they would be better off with me. So we went to Mississippi to stay with my folks and right before enough time passed for legal residency in the state, she hits me with an emergency hearing for custody."

"In New Hampshire?" the man asked.

"Yeah. Well, the judge there and the judge in Mississippi fought over the case and ultimately decided that the kids were still residents of New Hampshire. So I had to go back for a quick court date and when I did the New Hampshire judge said 'young children are better off with their mothers'. He gave me fourteen days to bring them back. That was in 1990. And I had to fight in court for every chance to see them for years because the judge that decided the custody case gave her sole custody."

"Why was that, Alan?"

"Hell if I know. She left us. She got this expensive ass lawyer known for winning custody battles for mothers. They even tried to get my lawyer to drop my case."

"How did they do that?"

"Her lawyer apparently told my lawyer, who was a woman, that I had tried to rape her when I came up for the initial custody hearing. Of course, I had to deny it to my attorney and explain myself…and when we went to court to finalize the divorce and custody, my lawyer brought it up in court in examination. Her lawyer and my ex both denied they ever said that. My attorney was dumb founded."

"So your lawyer was female. Was her lawyer a woman, too?" the man asked.

"No. Neither was the judge but he was confused by the conflicting statements and between that and all the women that they had accused me of sleeping with and me not having a job, because I was in school full time working on a medical degree, they fucked me over big time."

"Did you have extramarital affairs, Alan?"

"Nooo. I never cheated on the Bitch. Or at least not to fruition. I did have a brief encounter with an ex-girlfriend, but when it came down to the act, I froze up and couldn't go on with it. I kept thinking about my new baby. And I told the bitch what happened. Twelve years later she brings it back up in court. But I've never or even ever have been accused of ANY crime!"

"So why did any of that matter to the court?"

"Because you don't need proof in family court. Just hear-say. Her Mom and her friends went to court and lied on the stand. I was a

Southern boy in a Yankee Court. I didn't stand a chance up there."

"How often did you get to see your girls?"

"I saw them about four times total. From the time of the divorce that they were three and seven until my youngest was nineteen. Their Mom held my youngest back a grade so she could collect the extra year of child support. That is the damn truth. And I also had to pay for any and all expenses to see them per the divorce decree."

"You didn't live up there?"

"No. I had gotten a job as an orderly at a hospital in Jackson and was trying to go back to school for nursing. On one trip up North to fight for my visitation rights, I couldn't afford a lawyer so I represented myself. When I tried to question her on the stand, the judge said I wasn't asking the questions right and I had to stop. I asked how I was supposed to do it and he said he could not advise me. I also was about three weeks behind in child support and she counter sued for that with attorney fees. By the end of the day I was so distraught that I told the

Judge, *I will take my judgment from God himself—just like you and you and you*, and I pointed to the Bitch, her attorney, and the Judge."

"How did that go over, Alan?"

"Well, when I pointed to the Judge, he slammed his gavel down and pronounced me in *Contempt of Court* and gave me thirty days in jail. I served it in Hillsborough County up there. It put me in further financial distress. I kept getting behind in child support and never moved back up there as planned to be near my girls because I was afraid of being put back in jail for something. She always was threatening me with that jail shit. So, I had to borrow money to get a lawyer to enforce the visitation every time and then have them flown down for supervised visitation at my folk's house. I could never afford to see them. And I had to fight her every time I wanted to. The court never reprimanded her. It was always the same judge."

"Well, that explains your depression involving your children," the therapist stated. "How old are your girls now?"

"About thirty-three and twenty-seven."

"And do you see them now, Alan?"

"No. They don't even talk to me. It's been almost two years since we spoke. They got mad at me for something. Probably because I tried to state my case about what happened and why I couldn't see them more often when they were growing up. And I may have called their mother a cunt. When I was talking to them."

"It sounds like they are angry because they think you deserted them. What if you tried to tell them again, Alan? Just not in a way that would insult their mother."

"They won't hear a word of it. They have been told all their lives by their family up there that I am a bum and never wanted them. I know they blame me for not being there when they were growing up but I wasn't allowed to be. Their mother prevented it every time till they were out of her house. By then they really didn't remember me much. There was a time after that that we talked every few weeks and saw each other a couple of years until they just finally grew older and got caught up in their own adult lives. Their Mom totally has erased me out of their memory. They never got my letters or gifts because they said I never sent them anything when they were little."

"You don't think there is any hope in getting back together with them?"

"I think the circle is complete now," Alan said with his head bowed. I found out on Facebook that my oldest was pregnant. It was posted on her and her sister's pages. I found it through my brother's page. When I saw it, it was a couple weeks old already. She never told me. None of my family did. I deleted my account I was so upset. A few weeks ago, I was told by my Mom that she had a baby girl. My first grandchild. A baby girl. I had hoped that although I had not known my baby girls, that I would someday have a granddaughter. Looks like I do. But like I said, it has come full circle. Now my daughter will erase any knowledge of me from her daughter as well. I can't get my head around it."

There was a long pause in the room. The late morning sun was starting to fill the space with gentle golden rays. They flickered on the floor like those on the water just a few blocks away.

"Alan." The clinician started. "You are an Operation Urgent Fury Veteran, aren't you?"

"Yes. I was a Corpsman on *'The Moose'*—DD 980."

"And ya'll went ashore in Grenada?" the man asked.

"I did a couple times. Air lifts. We tended to some of the Marines and Cubans in the initial firefight. I also did some temp duty to help out with wounded coming in onto the Guam in the infirmary."

The man again scrolled through his electronic notes before asking, "Was your best friend there too? Another Corpsman."

"Sam? No, he had gotten off the ship a year and a half before. Took shore duty in Charleston when he re-uped'." Alan looked at the floor silently for a moment as contemplating a fading memory. "Sam was fuckin' my wife when I was patching up Commies and Jarheads. I didn't know about that until years later. He and the Bitch apparently had been screwing for a while.

Every time I went to sea that last year. Months on end. We kept up on My Space and Facebook for a while after we got out. Then one day he got 'born again'. Decided he needed to come clean with me. At first I thought he had married the cunt. He was from Mass'. Turned out to be a *real Masshole*. I knew she had remarried pretty quick. I didn't know who. She went so far as to have her husband take her last name just to keep it secret from me. And the girls were instructed to never speak of it. What a dumb bitch. I didn't give a fuck. I just wanted to see my kids."

"Was it him? Did she marry your friend?"

"No. Turns out it was just some other sucker from up there. I don't even know if they are still together. The girls hadn't mentioned him in a couple years. Don't care."

Both men were starting to fidget about in their chairs. The session had been longer than expected.

"OK Alan," the therapist started, "I wish you would consider getting back on some meds. I can get you an appointment with the Doctor to write a prescription under my advice. I think it would help you sleep better and take the edge off these nightmares. You already suffer from anxiety and maybe PTSD. I know you got into the program from your Primary Doctor's recommendation. Now that it has become an implemented standard to ask all Vets if they have had thoughts of suicide and hurting yourself or others, we are able to reach more like you. You were brave enough to answer the question honestly a few months ago, so let's move to the next stage." The man paused. "Are you thinking about hurting someone or yourself now, Alan?"

"Not at the moment. I just feel depressed. Sad. And I need these dreams to stop."

"The new meds will help with that."

"Stace has been wanting me to start back on them. It was her—my current wife that helped me get this far. I really appreciate her. I never realized I had a problem all these years. Just thought it was normal. Been called an asshole so many times for so many years, thought I was one—just cause I was."

"It's not uncommon for veterans *not* to

realize that they have some form of PTS until diagnosed. Many times, its years later when something like a suicide attempt or a tragedy happens. That's why the VA has started asking the questions about *suicidal feelings and the feelings of safety in your environment*. It is a standard question in every medical office visit now. And it sounds like you have a great support network at home too. And we have Anger Management group starting in a few minutes as well." The man finished typing on his computer as he spoke. "There is one other thing I want you to consider, Alan. I think it might be good to try to contact your daughters. Have you thought about it?"

"Yeah. My wife has been talking about it. I'm scared though. I don't wanna be rejected again. I don't want to have hope where there is none. I don't know if I can handle that."

"Well, think about it. Talk to Stacy about it. Ya'll decide. We can work through it together. Let's get you seen for the Doc. I can get you in tomorrow afternoon at 1400. Is that gonna work?"

"Yep. I'm off for a few days this week.

Rotation at the nursing home. They've been workin' us CNA's to death."

"OK good. Come by my office after you see the Doc and I'll get the meds expedited here so you won't have to wait so long in that pharmacy line."

"I appreciate that."

"Great. Let's go to group. And I'll see you again here in a couple weeks."

Alan was beginning to feel much better with the new meds. His anxiety was releasing and only after about twelve days of usage, his dreams had become more peaceful.

Stacy and Alan had spoken at length about the possibility of calling the girls. They knew it would be awkward and frightening. He had fought hard for years to see his children to little avail. This could backfire and be another disappointment in his life as well. But he thought about his options and considered what would be lost if he did not try. Alan thought, *at least I have another appointment scheduled with the Doc in couple more days if all else* *fail*s.

Stacy stood by Alan's side to comfort him when needed. Her soft hands caressed his lower back. With a clearer mind and trembling hands, Alan picked up the phone and dialed New Hampshire.

A familiar tender voice he had not heard in several months answered softly.

"Hey... it's Dad," he returned.

After a brief pause, the new mother let out an audible gasp—one of surprise, sadness and shame. But the phone line did not go dead.

Upon hearing this, Alan collapsed to his knees as he had done years before at his parent's home in the children's old bedroom. He had cried out loudly to God pleading, *where are my children*? Tears streamed down his face now as then. Neither he nor his daughter could speak as gulping sobs heaved each of their bodies violently. At this moment they were separated by 1500 miles of joyful pain, but only a breath apart.

Yet at the end of the line, another tiny breath was noted momentarily. It was one that Alan had never heard before—one of cooing and gurgling.

"You have a granddaughter, Dad. And we both love you so much."

TWO BISCUITS

"Grandma, that is the best stewed chicken I have ever smelled."

"Why thank you, Vlasta," Grandma said over a puff of flour in which her famous scratch biscuits were being kneaded.

"Will Grandpa be home on time for our special lunch today?" the gentle child asked excitedly. "He never takes his watch."

"Of course, dear—Grandpa needs only check the position of the sun. He always makes it home in time from the fields. I'm sure that today especially, that ol' tractor il' be putterin' on in right up to the back porch."

Grandma pulled a smudged white dish towel from beneath the strings of her blue and white checkered apron. She brushed her moist silver brow dry before loading a batch of egg washed biscuits into the hot oven.

"You know, your Grandpa's been lookin' forward to this meal for some time now. Every spring when we get the new pullets, I put a couple of the old layers in the fatt-nen' coop. After a couple weeks, Grandpa takes em' out and I cook em' up."

"Yeah, and it's gross when he cuts their head off and lets 'em run around the yard," the child snickered, reaching for a fresh baked apricot kolach.

"Well, never you mind that, young lady. And save some room for your lunch. Those pastry il' fill you up quicker'n your Grandpa fetch'n his glasses to watch the channel thir'teen weather girl."

Vlasta looked forward to visiting her grandparents Texas farm every spring vacation. It was an indication that soon summer would be here and regular visits to the Dime Box area were soon to come. The small Czech and German communities offered a host of exciting barbecues, homemade ice cream socials at the church and two-stepping for everyone at the SPJST lodge.

But the best part of the stay was always cooking with Grandma. She was known the county over for her baking skills. Grandpa always teased that is why he married her. But pictures taken of her forty years earlier showed a much different reason—her beauty.

"Honey, come take this scrap pot out the back porch for me, will ya?"

"Yes, Ma'am," the child answered. "Do you want me to take it out to the chickens now?"

"No, your Grandpa should be comin' in about ten more minutes. He won't wanna wait when he walks in and smells the biscuits browning. Sometimes he gets so excited, he forgets to say grace."

"Grandpa sure does like chicken and biscuits," Vlasta called as she pushed open the squeaky screen door to the porch.
"I don't see 'em yet, Grandma. And all's I hear is a Bobwhite calling and a Katie-did buzzin'. No tractor yet."

And that's when it hit her. If Grandpa was going to be late, why not play a joke on him. He was always fooling the two ladies with stories about how he saw a real live jack-a-lope in one of the pastures; or how he had struck oil while turning up rows with the tractor. Grandpa was a real character when it came to tall tales.

"Grandma. I have a great idea!" Vlasta shouted excitedly. She scampered back into the aroma filled kitchen. "Let's tell Grandpa we forgot to make his biscuits!"

"Where did you get such an idea?" Grandma asked smiling.
She continued to ladle the stewed chicken into an earthenware serving dish—stopping to wipe a stray splatter of gravy from the side.

"Well, Grandpa is always playin' jokes on us. So let's get 'em back."

"I suppose it would be funny. He won't even notice till he sits down and grabs his fork that there aren't any biscuits. I remember when we first got married, he had to have his chicken and biscuits every week—sometimes twice that week. I told 'em that if we didn't start eatin' the hogs and beef more often, we'd sprout feathers!"

So as it was the two playful vixens plotted their plan. And it was not long until the squeaky screen door burst open as Vlasta was placing the last glass of iced tea on the table.

"Boy, that smells good today. I wonder what it could be?" Grandpa asked knowingly.

"You're late, Grandpa," Vlasta blurted with a giggly smile.

"Well, you know, the sun took the day off today, and the moon took over. That means everything's backwards. Go see for yourself— must be midnight."

Grandpa quickly washed up and headed straight for the table passing Grandma by without even a mention of her. He sat down quickly, straightened his chair and called, "Two biscuits, please."

"Perhaps we could sit down and even say the blessing, sir," Grandma scorned.

It was just as she had predicted. Grandpa forgot everything on chicken and biscuit day. He didn't even notice the missing baked goods.

*"Thank-you-Lord-Jesus-for-this-day-our-food-our-health, annnd
-the-best-chicken-and-biscuits-in-the-county-Amen—two biscuits, please."*

Grandpa was not going to wait another

minute. He gave the blessing all in one breath.

"Lordy-sakes-alive!" Grandma exclaimed with both arms in the air. "I forgot to make biscuits this mornin' with all the bakin' we did."

Grandpa's eyes grew wide and his jaw dropped open as if it were to fall to his plate. With a knife in one hand and a fork in the other, his arms rested limp upon the table as if he had just finished parting the Red Sea. His forehead was wrinkled all the way up to his bald head. Grandpa looked as if he were about to cry.

The joke had worked just as planned. Grandma laughed so hard that she popped a button off of her blouse. Vlasta ran giggling into the kitchen and returned with the hidden hot plate of golden biscuits.

With Grandpa still trying to capture the years just stolen from his aging heart, Vlasta set the biscuits in front of him and threw both arms around his soiled and salty neck.

"We love you, Grandpa", Vlasta praised, yielding a soft kiss on her grandfather's bristly cheek. "We'd never forget your biscuits."

Grandma smiled and winked at him. Grandpa then picked up two biscuits. He broke them open releasing a gush of hot steam and an aroma of browned flour and buttermilk that was the best in the county. A smile from ear to ear lined his sun burned face. *This is what makes life grand*, he thought.

"Two biscuits, please," Vlasta echoed.

STRAYED

"Drake, come an' eat this bread right now," four year old Ivy demanded. "If you don't, you're going to be hungry."

The handsome English Caller drake had no intention of being disturbed this fine Indian summer day in early November. He was quite content to swim beneath the golden Sugar Maples and probe for tiny creatures in his cool New England brook.

"Drake. You can't go up there. Daddy and Mommy say no."

But Drake was not to be punished if he swam past the small clearing that Ivy's father had made to feed him from. Only moments before, the little girl's mother had run into the house to answer the phone. Ivy had been warned to *stand there—and keep away from the water*.

"Drake, you're in big trouble now. Come

back here," the young child called. But the bird's stylishly curled tail feathers only winked at her as she continued to throw pieces of stale bread after him.

"Mommy's mad at you, Drake" she said softly to herself. "You better come back here. We're both in trouble for you now."

Wearing her favorite pink and white knit sweater, the fair skinned child looked back at the open back door of the cedar-shingled Cape Cod home. Her mother was not in sight. The toddler gently stuffed the remaining two slices of coarse bread into her small red jean pockets. She wiped her hands neatly over the sweater's kitty design that Nana had made especially for her. Without a second thought, Ivy stepped from the safety of the clear landing and into the brushy bordering hemlock.

"Drake, you come here."

Drake had swum farther down the narrow brook, stopping occasionally to investigate the leafy shallow banks. Many treats were to be found in the watery compost. But Ivy drove the curious duck farther and farther down stream with her persistent pursuit.

"Ouch," Ivy scorned when her thin canvass tennis shoe stepped upon a crooked birch twig. It whipped up and struck her ankle smartly.

"Drake, that's too far. You don't know what's over there. It might be some monsters. You better stop."

The hardwood forest's partially bare canopy allowed the mid-afternoon sun to sprinkle splotches of silver sunlight upon the dark and somber undergrowth below. Large mossy boulders, unearthed by centuries of floods and frost heaves, sat silently—cold and grey, as the child passed their sentry into the forbidding dense wood.

"Drake, you can't go over that or you'll fall. It's too slippery—Daddy says!"

The fleeting fowl managed to scamper quickly around a mini babbling waterfall. Drake's stubby orange-webbed feet slid as if ice skating over the wet polished stone. Ivy's pink little fingers barely missed her cornered pet.

"Oooh-ahh!" Ivy scowled as she pulled herself from the soft ground on which she had fallen. "You got my hands and knees dirty." Ivy wiped the moist dark soil on the sides of her kitty sweater before looking back. She could no longer see the bright clearing she had left only moments ago. The forest was now beginning to look much larger and ominous to her. The air felt colder and she was sure she had heard her mother calling. It was scary.

Suddenly, a loud ratcheting from a branch above startled her. A noisy, little, Red Squirrel had been feeding on beech nuts before her intrusion. The small chattering animal put on a show of tail whipping and trunk scampering that made Ivy very afraid. In her fright, the young child unconsciously wet herself. She charged through the leaf littered wood wildly. Every step crunched evilly and small flocks of Chickadees darted swiftly before her. The ruckus scared Drake so silly that he flew several feet in front of her— quacking feverishly all the way.

"Drake, come back! You're gonna get lost." But the frightened duck continued waddling up the thinning trail of water. Ivy followed, not sure which way was back.

The forest yielded new secrets with every

straying step. Crimson and golden leaves fell quietly from the tall skyward trees. Small slithering salamanders scampered between rocks and brush. Overhead, birds and squirrels jumped from branch to branch in a percussion symphony of scratching and dancing boughs. The cool mountain air was sweet and tickled the toddler's pink nose. Ahead, the hardwood forest seemed to lighten in density.

The once babbling brook with cool pools of pristine water had far faded away as they traveled farther from home. The stream had now narrowed and all but disappeared. The two quickly found themselves in a wet grassy brown bog. Its edges were surrounded by red leafed Swamp Maples and Wild Cherry Trees. Old stumps lay rotting from previous harvest cuttings. The debris made travel difficult for the inexperienced child. She stumped her foot on obscured obstacles causing her to fall several times.

"Drake--I'm wet! And you just keep flying off," she sobbed. "Mommy's going to be mad with me."

The tall tawny grass reached for Ivy's

waist and thin ice crackled as she journeyed on. Cold and muddy water squished vehemently in her small soaked shoes, until they crossed to a drier basin on the other side of the bog. It was mostly free of trees. But the exposed autumn sun gave no refuge to the shivering child.

A forgotten crumbling stone wall bordered the far side of the swamp. Drake had flown to it and sat grooming himself as if to wait for Ivy to reach her goal. She could see a thick host of green Balsam Fir trees behind the bird. It looked like Christmas to her and Santa came to mind. Perhaps she was near his house. He would certainly help. But within a few yards of reaching the bulwark, her feet stuck solidly in a patch of soft sucking mud.

"Help! Help me…Mommy!" the child screamed hysterically. But no one heard the helpless toddler's tearful cry. It was as if the greedy ground had turned into a hidden scary monster—pulling her down, down, down.

The child managed to grab clumps of grass in front of her and wiggle free after minutes of timely terror. She emerged shoeless. When Ivy reached the stacked stone barrier, the child climbed up only to see Drake waddling off again. She reached into her tight wet pants pocket and scraped out a small handful of sticky bread mush to offer him. The tiny trembling hand could not coax him back.

"Drake, come back. Come here. Please come back," she begged. But the bird remained idle under aromatic evergreens further up the bank.

As Ivy sat in the sun resting upon the cold granite stones, a large black crow flew closely overhead cawing loudly. The young child quickly hopped off of the rickety rocks. She hid herself briefly from the inquisitive boisterous bird before approaching the duck for comfort. Within inches of grasping his neck, Drake once again flinched away.

Ivy reluctantly followed him into the twiggy fir grove ahead. It was darker and much cooler than the hardwood forest. Several low hanging dead twigs seemed to leap at her face. They scratched often and toyed with her long tangled hair. Earlier, the sun had shown brightly by the edge of the brook at home. Her matching pink knit hat which had been left there now could have warmed her ever reddening ears. That was not to be.

Fallen fir needles cushioned the forest floor like a thick carpet. But it was of little comfort. Being shoeless, she was subjected to their desiccated sharp points. The child's wet cotton socks picked the needles up by the dozens which began to spear her tender feet with every step. She spent the next traveling hour stopping, sitting and brushing off prickles before continuing to follow the avian wanderlust.

Highest fanning boughs captured most of the comforting sunlight. This made the lesser few feet of each evergreen to appear to be dead. Only jagged stark stems extended from the lower tree trunks that looked like an elephant's skin. Ivy was just the right height to be able to see through the bare branches. Eventually, a second stone wall greeted her eyes from yards away; as did curious slate-blue colored Nuthatches—wondering what a child of this age was doing alone in this part of the wood.

When Ivy reached the old lichen covered boundary, the light grew brighter. The forest edges changed to towering short leafed pines. These trees were spaced quite well apart unlike those in the previous woods. It seemed the forest was to allow her to escape. The weary child walked briskly toward the illuminance leaving the wayward bird behind.

"Come on, Drake. It's too scary here," she cried from the shadows.

Drake flew from the white speckled wall to within a few feet in front of her. An azure sky opened farther ahead.

"Do you see sumthin', Drake?" Ivy asked breathlessly with tiny arms swinging in the air as she marched on. "I think it's our house."
But the closer they got to the edge of the wood, no houses could be seen.

The trees parted into a vast sloped clearing. With exit in sight, Ivy began to forget about the scary monsters behind her only to be surprised by the shrill clatter of a large Pileated woodpecker that was returning to its roost. The frightened and shrieking child bolted from the dark wood with damp socks flapping before her every step. She tumbled forward into a crimson veil of wild blueberry fields bathed in late afternoon sun. The small shrubs gently cushioned her fall.

Wet, cold, soiled and scraped, the exhausted toddler huddled at the bottom of a large weathered boulder near the middle of the meadow. She soon fell asleep, sobbing—sucking her dirty but trusted thumb. The sun continued to set. The air grew ever colder. Puffy clouds in the dusk sky glowed with red and orange. The pair had been gone for a long time. Ivy was a missing child on a rural New England mountainside in November.

The vista from the rolling hill on which the child lay gave view to an oblong lake edged by fiery colored trees indicative of the season. Behind her, not more than forty yards above, Radio Tower Road intersected with her sheltering refuge on Hatchet Mountain's base route. Farthest in the eastern distance, over Payson's Apple Orchards, Maine's mid-coast mountains could be seen kissing the sea.

"Ivy! Ivy!" a strained voice cried. Warm strong hands grasp the child's leaf-matted sweater and shook her passionately from above.

"Daddy."

"Geez, Dee-a'—are you OK?"

"Ayuh. But where's Drake?" she asked lethargically.

"He's right here. He was sittin' next to you—snuggled up. Lord child, you scared your mother and me to death. She's gone crazy looking for you—the whole town of Hope's in the woods!"

"Daddy, please don't spank me," the child suddenly sobbed, tears gushing.

"Sweet Baby, I'm not going to spank you. I'm not mad with you. Let's go home and see your Mommy—we love you precious child."

Her father sighed deeply, cradling her tightly to his warm chest. He wrapped her snuggly under his oversized flannel coat before heading up the hill to the rest of the search party.

"Now let's get home."

"And Drake, too?" she asked.

"And Drake, too" he comforted.

EBT DOWN

2 Thessalonians 3:10 KJV *"For even when we were with you, this we commanded you, that if any would not work, neither should he eat."*

"Oooooooo Granny…can we get some Mountain Dew? It's on sale! Two twelve packs for buy one get one free."

The thin statured, graying, late fifties grandmother was reaching into the refrigerated case to obtain a white gallon of store brand milk marked 2% reduced fat. Her mind was not on soda. She was concentrating on a strict shopping list. According to the store flyer, a purchase of two of these products would enable her to buy a dozen eggs for ninety-nine cents— with her value savings card. *That will be one more item on the list that will help my budget*, she thought.

The neatly dressed woman turned to the basket with her acquired items. She directly faced the animated eight-year-old child standing in front of an end cap filled with hyper-colored green and red ready-for-fridge packs. Their box graphics were sharp and edgy. The floor was stacked over shelf crest high and end aisle wide. A retro looking Frankenstein's monster door decoration had been added to the display with a sale sign in his hand. It gazed back at her.

"Honey, you know we have a budget," the grandmother said. She thought to herself despairingly, *we made it past the candy displays, but they still try to get you in the milk aisle.*

"Please Granny," the little girl begged as she had earlier in the store. "Granpop likes it, too. And we haven't had any for awhile. It's on sale, Granny."

The lady sighed and remembered her own daughter years before in trips to the grocery just like this one. The only thing different was that times were better then. Steady pay checks had been in order. And there had been little concern for strict budgets. But now things had changed. This time it wasn't her daughter she was trying to corral around the blatant child-marketing displays—shrewd exhibits that had been strategically placed in the back of the store. It was her deceased daughter's child. The court had granted custody to them three years ago when her mother was killed on an icy road over Bays Mountain. Perhaps that is why she said, "Grab two. But you and Granpop gotta make-do with them for quite a while."

"We will," the spry wisp of a girl confirmed.

Other than the irritation of a wayward shopping cart wheel, the remainder of the trip was fairly uneventful. Granny was able to fulfill her grocery list. She had carefully planned necessities with sale items, coupons and allowable items pretty much *'to a T'*. All they had to do now was navigate the busy checkout lines.

It was only a minute or two after Eleven A.M. when Granny and her granddaughter began to place their items on the register belt. Beatrice, a tall dark haired woman with a crisp uniform and a manager's badge, took the regional chain stores value card from the young girl's hand as the grandmother had instructed. Stoically the woman scanned it quickly and handed it back to the child. The cashier then continued to scan the items with as much efficient harmony as the repetitive resounding symphony of electronic beeps filling the store's bustling exit lines.

Upon ringing up the last item, Granny gave the woman a small stack of coupons. She noticed the manager's fingertips were slightly yellowed and a strong odor of cigarette smoke was evident as the two women came closer together for the exchange. The smell was common in this part of Appalachia. Southwestern Virginia and the Tri-cities area were locally known for tobacco growth and use. It also boasted nearby Country Music and NASCAR attractions.

The mid-thirties cashier had a big hair style that any female Grand Ole Opry singer would envy. A red and black key lanyard with the number 3 hung halfway out of her pants pocket. Granny couldn't help but think that the junior woman must have really been a pretty girl in earlier years, but that heavy smoking was beginning to cause deep lines in her face. The older woman just smiled at her younger counterpart before she slid her EBT card through the payment processor when directed.

"Try it again," the manger ordered.

Granny did as told. She entered her PIN once more with a quizzical look on her brow. She knew about how much she had left on the card. This was only her second trip to the store this month. She had been quite frugal with her spread out spending.

The cashier gave a disgruntled look to the register's computer screen. It was then that a bagger from another line came up to her and said, "Miss Beatrice, we have a problem on number seven with a food stamp card."

"Hang on," she snapped back at the employee. The manager then typed a few more keys before addressing Granny with "give me a moment, ma'am." With that the cashier stepped a few feet away from the register and pulled a small black phone from her pants pocket. She spoke quietly into it for what seemed to be several minutes.

A bright faced boy with a short cropped hair smiled at Granny. He had meticulously placed the woman and her granddaughter's items in plastic bags. Even though the store had been bustling and the lines were starting to fill, he had been attentive in his work. The older woman returned the smile and thought well of him.

"The EBT system is down. Do you have another way to pay?" the manger asked coldly on her return.

"I don't have a credit card or anything like that," Granny replied coyly. "How long do you think it will be down?"

"I have no idea, ma'am. But if you want this you need cash."

Granny helped the cordial bag boy retrieve an off-brand box of fish sticks, one of the gallons of milk and a loaf of white bread. She paid for those items with cash. The remainder of the thoughtfully bagged groceries was left in the cart. As the young man wheeled the abandoned basket to a restocking area away from the busy checkout lines, he thought about his own needs for the evening. Turning around, he almost bumped into the bagger with register seven's denied order.

"Hey, Swiss cheese!" a burly voice blurted as a tow headed little girl hopped in his lap.

"Granpop…why do you always call me that?"

"Well. 'Cause my eyes are kinda funny and I see spots. When I look at you and your pretty golden hair you look like Swiss cheese."

"Granpop, you're silly." The little girl gave her Grandfather a big kiss on his scruffy cheek and jumped down to go play in her room.

"Granny, you need some help with the

groceries?" the man asked.

"No. I'm afraid not," she answered unemotionally. The food stamp machine was down at the store and I couldn't get much."

"Was down? How does that happen? I've never heard of such," the man said as he turned toward the grandmother in the kitchen.

"Yeah. I don't know but they aren't sure how long it will be broken. I don't know what I'm gonna be able to take for the pot-luck at church tomorrow."

The couple's little Catholic church was celebrating their priest's first anniversary there. Though he served several small congregations in his parish, each one of the flocks had planned a modest meal to show their appreciation. This event was welcomed by the young rector because he would be blessed with leftovers for hot meals throughout the month when each congregation had its own event.

"Well. It won't be the first time we didn't bring somethin' fancy," Granpop said.

It had been almost seven years since the man had been laid off from Eastman in Kingsport. Granpop had driven a truck locally after his four year service in the Navy as a Seabee. Sixteen years later, just before his fortieth birthday, he finally got a coveted job at the chemical plant. He had hoped that it would do well for his family's retirement. But in almost as many years as it took to get hired on there, his career ended due to labor cuts. Fortunately, he was able to payoff the mortgage of their modest house in the Gate City area soon after acquiring that of which was his last gainful employment.

Granny had been a housewife and mother to their only daughter. But when her husband had been laid off she eventually went to work out of necessity. The VA in Johnson City had helped pay for Granpop's heart attack a year after his work had ended. And it was now helping him with a recent diagnosis of diabetes. But when she lost her job at the battery plant in Bristol a year and a half ago, things started to get worse for them.

"The college radio had a show on today talking about food deserts," the man started. "At least we have a place to get groceries."

"A what?" Granny asked as she spread

mayonnaise on bread for bologna sandwiches.

"A food desert. It's a place where they don't have good markets. For people in big cities like Detroit. All they have are maybe a couple of small corner stores or convenience stores for folks to get food at. Most don't have fresh foods, just chips and vee'annie sausages I guess."

"They don't have grocery stores in Detroit?" Granny asked incredulously.

"Yeah, they have 'em, but most are in the suburbs. They say it's not profitable for chain groceries to open up in the poorer inner city neighborhoods. And small groceries can't make it either. Some places like father up in the mountains have the same problem."

"Lord tell," Granny expressed. "With all this nation has, it won't even feed its own people. We are blessed." The woman looking ages beyond her years from burden gazed up at the wall above the kitchen table. There was a crucifix with a suffering Jesus and a photo of Pope Francis below it. She said a silent prayer to herself and made the sign of the cross about her.

"Yes, we are blessed, Dear. But if these Republicans get this big cut in food stamps they want passed with the Farm Bill, then we may have a food desert in our own house. Sometimes I wonder if we shouldn't have just voted for Obama."

"Granpop! You know we vote for Christian values."

"I do. But don't you like to quote Pope Francis when we have had to go to the food bank and they ask you if you've been saved? It makes you angry because we don't believe that way. You always say, "the Pope preaches that the Church should be like the moon—reflective of the source of God. Not thinking it is God himself." If being affiliated with a certain political party means being godly, then maybe we are lost."

Granny stopped setting the table at that statement. She thought to herself, Granpop will be sixty-two in a few months. Maybe he will be able to draw social security. All of the SSI applications for him had been denied so far, and her unemployment was fast running out. With the end of the year looming quickly, there was talk that the extension of benefits would not be renewed. Granny considered her husband's words profoundly.

"God is good," the woman said as she placed glasses of milk on the table. "Today we have been provided for. Tomorrow we will not be forgotten either—just like the birds of the air. Go get our grandbaby and let's rejoice in His name over this meal that has been provided for us this day."

The cordial bag boy with the bright face who had bundled Granny's groceries stepped inside of the small cabinet maker's shop. His apartment room was upstairs. He, his wife and daughter found refuge there. It was her Aunt and Uncle that rented them the one room attic space. If not for them, they would certainly be on the street by now.

The couple was a statistical stereotype of rural children having babies. When he was a high school Senior and she a Junior, the Abstinence Programs did little to persuade the uneducated lovers. They became parents of a beautiful baby girl by mid-term school year. The boy graduated but the new mother dropped out.

Her father's religious convictions had led him to *condemn and cast out'* the pregnant girl from her childhood home once her secret was evident. He was a deacon in the Greater Victory Missionary Baptist Church. So ardent were his beliefs that he allowed no family member to stray from his word as family leader. It was her mother's sister who offered the girl sanctuary in their home.

An agreement was made that if the lovers married before the baby was born, they could stay with the extended family. Her Uncle sufficiently remodeled a loft storage space above his small work building in town. Existing lighting and electric fixtures were reclaimed. Insulation was added to the sloping rafters and enclosed with sheet rock. The two old windows were reconditioned and screens were added.

A compact stove and an old refrigerator were arranged in a newly enclosed room downstairs. A single dish sink was plumbed with existing water lines from the shop's bathroom which they shared with the business. The man also added a metal shower stall next to the toilet facilities.

For winter's heat the uncle inserted a single floor register connected to existing duct work. An open deck grill allowed return air from the above space. The placement of this hole disseminated noise from the oil furnace's motor and boisterous visitors from below. But the young couple was grateful. His divorced mother had no room for them in her small Kingsport flat.

"Hey Babe. Did you remember to get the cake mix and ice cream?" a slightly chubby young mother asked. She was holding a wiggly round faced baby girl in her arms. Her smile was as big as her Daddy's when their eyes meet.

"The food stamp machine was broke today. Miss Beatrice told people all day that they had to pay cash or put it back." The young man opened a small bag and placed a twin pack of Swiss rolls and a personal serving container of chocolate ice cream on the bed. "I only had three dollars. So I got this."

As the girl gave the reaching baby to her father, she asked "How long is it gonna be broke?" She then picked up the items and turned to go downstairs.

"I'm not sure. I didn't ask. I don't want Miss Beatrice knowing we use food stamps. I checked out in the self service line because she was still there before I left to walk home. It still wouldn't take the card."

When the couple reached the tiny kitchen, the girl placed the ice cream in the freezer. She took a t-shirt and sweat pants from a basket of freshly washed clothes sitting on the table. The basket was then moved underneath. Her soiled CNA scrubs were stripped off before replacing them with the new outfit she had decided upon.

"Well, I get paid on Tuesday from the nursing home. It should be about seventy-three hours. How many hours do you have this pay period?" the girl asked her husband.

"I should have the same forty hours. They never let me work more than twenty a week."

"We should get enough for gas and bill money for me to get to Kingsport to work for the next two weeks. Till we get paid again. I wish they would let you work more," she commented.

"I do too. But I should be leaving next month for boot camp. The recruiter said he will let me know for sure this week when I'm gonna leave."

"As long as they don't send you to Afghanistan. They did say that they are definitely pulling people out, right?" she asked looking directly into his eyes with concern.

"That's what he told me. He said the Army was pulling out and only leaving a few Marines. But Obama has a plan to get everyone home. That's what he said." The boy said it in a way that he was trying to convince himself as much as his young wife. "But we'll be better off, Babe. We should be off food stamps by Christmas. And you can get your GED and go to nursing school."

The girl put her hands out to her garbling one year old. The child grasped her mother's fingers and squealed joyfully but would not leave her father's hip.

"We are gonna have a better life than this.

We might even get the baby baptized."

"You mean sprinkled?" the young mother exclaimed with a comical look of puzzled doubt on her face.

"That's what y'all call it," the boy said.

"That's what you Methodists do. Y'all sprinkle babies," she asserted.

The young woman began to laugh but then an old memory befell her thoughts. It had been her freshman year in high school when her father required her to attend a funeral at their church. Her Dad was the officiating deacon for a two year old boy that had died from cancer. She would never forget his words to the grieving family members during the service. *'It is too bad that this child will go to Hell because it was not baptized and saved. But no one can question God's Will.'* Those words had haunted her from then on. She soon questioned *the word of God* as she had been taught.

"Well. Maybe we *can* sprinkle her," she said reconsidering.

"Hey. Are we gonna celebrate this child's first birthday or not?" the boy asked gleefully changing the subject. "Where's your

Aunt? Are they gonna celebrate with us?"

"No. They had to go to the church. It's Homecoming over there and they're settin' up. They're gonna do a foot washin' service."

"Homecomin'? Is your Mom gonna go?" the boy asked.

"I think she might. My Dad lets Mama go to that every year. He won't go. He doesn't like those kinda Baptists. I thought I might go, too, so I can see her. And bring the baby."

"I think you should," he comforted.

The room was quiet for a moment. The only sound was of wiggly feet trying to get down from her father's transitioned hip.

"Well, let's get this party started!" the young Mama proclaimed.

The teen couple proudly prepared the Swiss rolls on a plastic blue dinner plate. They got a metal spoon to share the ice cream between the three of them, and a butter knife to cut the cake. The father did not have a birthday candle so he took a kitchen match from the furnace room. Once he had struck it, the proud young Dad stuck the flaming wood into the cake. The parents immediately began to sing

"Happy Birthday to You, Happy Birthday…"

Before Beatrice could leave the store, she needed to pick up a few groceries. Her overnight guest was expected around eight. She had three hours to get home to prepare dinner and drink.

As the woman emptied her hand basket at the checkout, she remembered that she had forgotten the soda for her son. Beatrice spied a line of grocery baskets filled with items that some had not the means to pay for. She grabbed two twelve packs of Mountain Dew, and a large bag of potato chips for good measure from the abandoned baskets.

There was only one more errand to run. The trip to McDonalds was on her way to her parent's house in Kingsport. She ordered a ten piece Chicken McNugget with barbeque sauce for her twelve year old son Jacob and a large Coke for herself. It was early to the start of the evening meal, so the drive-thru wait was brief. Moments later she returned to the place she had dropped Jacob off on her way to work earlier that morning.

"I'm sorry dear, but this boy won't eat much of anything else but McDonald's. I don't know why you don't make him eat like everyone else does. These kids shouldn't be eating all this fast food stuff all the time," a lady in her early sixties scowled.

"Mom, he likes it and it's easy for me to get for him. Thanks for callin' me. It's not a problem," the younger woman said.

"Well, he's been good. Just watching TV and playing that video box thing with the snow skiing."

"It's called a Xbox. And he has the snowboarding game here."

"Well, he's been playing it most of the day. Papaw has been working all day so I didn't mind. I just don't like that zombie game thing he brought over. Your father had a fit over that last week," the older woman chided.

"His Dad got that for him. I won't let him bring it over anymore. It stays at home."

"Well good. It was too bloody and scary and loud." The grandmother took the bag of food from her daughter and continued to the kitchen. "So are you going to pick Jacob up after church tomorrow?"

"I'm going out with the girls tonight. I will pick him up later in the afternoon. I have a day off tomorrow."

The graying lady looked at the floor before returning her eyes to the younger woman. "I wish you would take time to come to church. Just 'cause you're saved doesn't mean you have any business running around in bars and drinking and smokin' when you like."

"I'm going out with a couple of friends to the movies, and probably Wild Wings. It's not a bar; it's a restaurant. And yes, I am gonna have some wine."

"Well, I think you should come with us more often. Pastor was asking about you and how your divorce is comin'. He said you need some counseling and I agree."

"Momma, I've been going to that church since I was a child. I remember when Pastor was just a Deacon. He's moved along in the world and so have I. My soon-to-be ex-husband is a sailor who I need to move along from, too.

I still have my Christian values, but I don't need everyone in Mount Carmel knowing all of my business. That's why I live in Virginia and go to church up there when I do."

"Well, I don't mean to upset you. We just worry about you, Honey."

"I know you do, Momma."

After assuring her mother that she would at least have Jacob go with them for *Trunk or Treat* at their church's Harvest Festival in a couple of weeks, she kissed her son good-bye and left. Beatrice took Lee Highway to her house just off of Old Dominion Road in Bristol. The ride took not more than a half hour. The four bedroom ranch style house was inviting and spacious.

Upon entering, the woman placed the groceries on the table. She opened a fresh bottle of wine as it was her daily custom to do so. Sutter Home was her preferred brand of drink. Benson & Hedges was her smoke. Both pleasures were readily available on the kitchen table as she began to strip off her work clothes. The local evening news at six o'clock was just starting when she turned on the television. In a few moments she would wash the day away with a hot shower.

The water was warm and comforting. It fell over her body with childhood memories of summer rain. Beatrice had been careful to cover her hair with a shower cap that made her think of her mother. *Speaking of,* she thought, *how dare she question my plans for the evening. I wasn't truthful, but it was not anyone's business but my own.*

The woman had no intention of meeting friends for a girl's night out. She had another plan in place. The fact was that her husband of thirteen years was out at sea for another few months on a naval aircraft carrier. He seemed to be more devoted to the Navy than her and her son. She understood that he was a pilot and that he was working his way up the ranks quickly by taking on as many long cruises as he could, but she was tired of being a Sea Widow. Beatrice had filed for divorce, transferred her management position to be as close to her family as she could and left her husband.

She was lucky to be able to find a job in Southwest Virginia, albeit in the small rural town of Weber City. Staying in the state would not complicate the custody situation. Her husband was stationed in Norfolk. Virginia law dictated that a married couple be physically separated for at least one year before divorce. Even though it was an *at fault state*, her attorney had assured her that judges commonly gave exception to the rule if the couple had been physically separated for at least that amount of time. It had been fourteen months. If that was not enough, the attorney would threaten the sailor with abandonment or adultery. It would be easy to find some evidence of multiple affairs involving the sojourning seaman, they thought. Either way, Beatrice was headstrong on ending the marriage. And she expected a good child support ruling as well as shared pension benefits from her husband's career. It was only a matter of time before he returned from sea to face the courts.

By the time she finished primping in the bathroom, the national news was broadcasting. Beatrice turned on the oven to bake a family pack of frozen macaroni and cheese. Stuffed pork chops acquired before leaving would be roasted in increment fashion to further her ease. A quart of peach cobbler from the deli could be microwaved to supplement the meal. All she needed do now was relax till her guest arrived.

Rounding out the day's news headlines were stories of the war in Syria, a GOP stop gap measure discussed in meetings with the President that Senators John McCain and Susan Collins reported as being "constructive" and a story about an NFL player's two year old son who had died after injuries from suspected abuse at the hands of his mother's boyfriend. But it was the mention of the day's EBT shutdown that caught her attention the most.

"Obama wants to give it all away," she cursed loudly at the television. "Well, good luck with that, you Muslim tyrant." Beatrice downed her third glass of wine and got up to pour herself another. She was thoroughly disgusted with the day's events.

First, it was the "entitled," she verbalized. Then it was her mother. *People just need to do for themselves, mind their own business and get a life*, she thought. She had worked hard for all she had. Why shouldn't everyone else? Stop making excuses. It was as clear as the open bible she had on her foyer table.

Beatrice checked on the oven dishes. She looked at the clock. The chops were ready to be put in. It was time to turn the *idiot box* off. Tonight would be another night of much needed company. With the evening's third lit cigarette and a fresh glass of wine, the resolute woman headed to the designated study of the four bedroom house. She turned on the computer. Above it was a picture of an angel with an inscription that read, *All things are possible in Christ*. In another corner of the room was a large poster of the inspirational poem, *Footprints in the Sand*.

It was getting close to seven-thirty when Beatrice had finished checking her email. She then logged into Facebook. It was here that she had reconnected with a high school friend from years ago. Her friend had done well and built a promising mineral rights law office in Abington. She knew her guest would be arriving before long. The woman was ready.

Perfume had been dabbed in all the most of intimate places and the Victoria's Secret after hours satin pajamas adorned her slim body. It promised to be another sensuous overnight. One of many enjoyed covertly over the past few months.

An electronic *Achy Breaky Heart* ringtone disturbed her social media posting. "Hey therrrrre," she cooed. "Ok. Yep, I'm here. No, just come on." She giggled. "Ok. See ya in a minute. Byyyyyyyye." Beatrice felt a tingle. It was a precursor to what was to be felt sooner than later. At the thought of the evening's desires, she became hot and flush. She had only one more thought before she was to leave and prepare for the night's activities.

It was the day's events that inspired her to type out on her Facebook page, *Sorry for those of you who's EBT card didn't work today...I'd have given you $5 to feed your babies...but you're gonna have to put back that 24-pack of Mountain Dew...time to get real!* And with that she clicked POST.

WATER RIGHTS

It tasted like dirt. Everything did. But the worst part was that it was the air. The air tasted like dried-up dirt. *Too bad we can't drink it*, Felicia thought. *We might be able to survive another winter season if we could.*

The clouds on the horizon were dark and purple. Incoming wind smelled sweet like ozone. It blended with foul, stale air. Another storm was forming. It brought promise of the rains. The red, cracked earth begged for such a nutrient. But it was unlikely to fall here. The drought in this part of central Tennessee had persisted for almost eleven years. Felicia remembered her grandparents saying that starting in the 30's, the drought had lasted for almost twice that long.

It was now the 70's. Her grandchildren had never known life above ground. The storms had gotten so bad in the late 20's that PermaCorp-Gov had begun to build underground dwellings on a massive scale. The quasi-governmental organization was formed for "national security reasons", citizens were told. Tornados had devastated much of the Midwestern United States by then. Massive hurricanes on the Gulf and East Coasts added to the misery. The nation's great interior migration, forty years before, only added to the depletion of resources.

New York City, New Orleans and San Francisco had disappeared by 2040. The collapse of the Antarctic ice sheets had contributed to the city's demise many years before. They were completely abandoned. Some say that over one hundred years ago, a former American president called Carter gave warnings about the need for natural resource conservation. He was echoed by historical figures named Gore and Obama. In her old age,

Felicia now wished that the people existing then would have put more faith in their fellow man. Instead, they blindly followed politicians, employing corporations, and even their savior religions.

The air was much fresher above ground. The close, dirty living quarters below were unbearable. Body heat amplified the conditions of overcrowding. Functioning, underground sewers had long been replaced by slop buckets that were emptied topside into open pits nearby. Outside, open defecation was common. It had further contaminated the top soil—a pollution problem of many countries once called "third world" in the twentieth century. Only the affluent had compost toilets. Flush commodes were extinct.

Even without the drought, growing crops topside would be difficult in the toxic soil. Much of the plant based diet was grown underground hydroponically, and aided by solar electricity. It still was not enough to feed everyone. The poorer servant communities suffered. Dysentery and cholera were rampant there.

Felicia's drab head cover was dusty and flapped in the hot breeze. The ailing woman sat on thick concrete. The outcrop was near an exposed portion of the development's water-pipe corridor. Its protective bunker was massive.

She could hear the rush of desalinated water being channeled to the larger city core by the massive pumps below. Felicia wondered if her community would receive their ration this week. They had been shorted in the past few deliveries. Violence had increased among the residents who lived beneath the earth. Everyone fought for the limited resource as it was inefficiently distributed. Riot officers from the Water Resources Unit often stood back in fear for their own lives.

The PermaCorp-Gov elite citizens were scheduled to receive their rations first. Although everyone in the world was in the same global predicament, it always seemed the more affluent residents were the first to be served. Historically, nothing had changed in this once great and respected, democratic country.

An immense, worldwide migration had started in 2031. Resources were limited; borders were overrun. Those with money and influence began to bunker down and form militarized, gated communities. These "communities" later became small, guarded, subterranean cites--especially after the country once known as North Korea blew itself up. They had launched a nuclear attack with ICBM missiles at Japan. The guidance software proved to be defective.

Many Western world leaders suspected that the Chinese had sabotaged the North Korean's launch programming. Others believed that theory to be untrue. Regardless, the residual radiation poisoned much of the East. It was turned it into a wasteland where an already water stressed region existed. After the United States abandoned Northern Africa and the Middle East, those countries also completely disintegrated from political turmoil and decades of war.

Global warming had already decimated countries known as India, Bangladesh and Pakistan during those pivotal, early years. Now forty years later, Felicia knew little of the history of her planet. Pollution, corporate greed and mismanagement of natural resources had caused the collapse of over half of the earth's nations and her indigenous population.

Large drops of sporadic rain fell on the ground before her. It looked as if puffs of smoke had wisped from the hell below. Felicia gazed to the north. Golden, stunted, ripples of speargrass waved back at her. The storms were building. Any amount of rain would be insignificant in refilling the long, depleted aquifers. Most everyone returned to the safety of the underground, but she remained.

The hail started to fall. The woman now in her early fifties heard the great steel doors close. She had ignored the warnings to come back in. Instead, she stood up from her resting place and methodically walked northward.

Large ice pellets pelted her back and head. Felicia picked up a dirty, red, ice stone from the arenaceous earth and put it into her mouth. The melting water tasted like the acidic sea, but it was cool and it refreshed her dry mouth despite the smell of reconstituted feces.

She mindfully savored the treat until a mass the size of a baseball knocked her into unconsciousness. Her body fell to the moistened clay. Felicia's goal to experience this blissful moment before she *left this wretch of an existence* was reached.

Hail continued to strike at her where she lay. The clouds gathered ever menacingly above. No one came to her aid. They had seen this act many times before. Chances were that she would not even be there once the doors had reopened. They were right. Her lifeless body was lifted up unceremoniously by the massive, cyclonic winds and carried far away from the dystopian community.

DO LIKE YOUR MAMA TOLD YA

It was hot. Al had not turned on the air conditioning to cool the car down; nor, had he opened the windows before Betty took her place next to him in the front passenger's seat.

"Al, I'm rolling this window down. It's hot in here," she said.

"You're gonna let all the cold air out. I cranked it up."

Betty rolled her eyes. After forty-two years of marriage, she knew he was not one to argue with. Her husband was one of the most stubborn old men she knew. She loved him, but his frugal ways were becoming more extreme as he aged. Now in their mid-sixties, Betty had hoped retirement would make him more tolerable.

"Did you remember the list? We need the list," Al directed.

"Yes, Honey, I brought the list," she returned in her sweetest, sarcastic voice. Al did not notice the aural embellishment.

"Did you put down birdseed? And how much toilet paper do we have? We have to make sure we have enough toilet paper."

"Alfred. You have a whole, hall closet full of toilet paper. You won't run out anytime soon."

"Well, probably not since you don't use it. I don't know why we have to have two kinds of toilet paper in our house," the man replied.

"You know I'm not gonna use your old, crappy brand of tissue. That stuff is like rough-hewn plywood. I don't know why you insist on buying the cheapest toilet tissue ever made on God's green earth."

"Well, it worked OK when I was in the Air Force. We were lucky to have something to wipe with in Nam. And after a day of door gunnin', sometimes we appreciated the sturdiness of a sheet to clean up with."

"OK, Sarge, let's just get back to the list. I've heard all of your poop-in-the-pants Nam stories—fallin' out of this chopper, hanging out of that one. They became even more festooned every time you told them to our boys when they were young."

Al was careful to survey his surroundings. The military had taught him that. *Traffic isn't so bad today*, he thought. *For a Saturday morning, it's lighter than usual.*

"The grand-babies are coming this week. Do we have enough cookies and stuff, or are you going to bake some? I like those soft bake ones at the Target," Al inquired.

"No, I'm going to bake some. They like my own peanut butter recipe best," Betty replied with a smile on her face.

"Yeah, I do too. You know that's why I married you."

"Alfred, the only reason you married me is because you like round bottoms and large breasts. Now you have even more to love. Thanks to the years."

Al grinned. He reached across for his

bride's hand, picked it up, and kissed it as he leaned toward her. He never took his eyes off of the road. It was a gesture he had made to her often.

"And that's why I married you. Because despite all of your orneriness, you can still be romantic and gentle," Betty cooed.

"It's all about you, Babe," Al replied smugly.

"Well. Then I do need some peanut butter." Betty turned her attention back to her list. Al continued to navigate to their first errand stop. "And I need some new panties. These are getting worn. And speaking of," she continued.

Al frowned. He knew what was coming next. He had heard it before. An audible sigh escaped his lips before he could catch himself.

"And speaking of," Betty repeated. "You could use a few new pairs as well."

A traffic light stopped Al only yards before his department store destination. There was nothing he could do at this point, other than listen to his wife moan about his underwear.

"My drawers are fine. I like them. They fit good and I don't need to be spending money on new, expensive tighty-whities. I can still wear them," the gray haired man insisted.

"Those things are so ratty, not even anyone in the Poor House would be caught wearing 'em. I'm embarrassed for you to even walk around the house in them. Now you best plan on getting a couple new pairs, or I'll throw them away myself and you'll be walking around half-nekid," Betty said sternly.

"No you won't. These are just fine. And besides--if you do, I *will* just go to town floppin' around nekid."

"Alfred Leon Baker! I know you weren't drug up; you had a proper raisin'. Now do like your mama told ya'. You have a big old hole in one pair that shows some of your business hanging out," Betty replied. *"Thing looks like a turkey wattle dangling down to your knees,"* she added, softly muttering to herself.

"What? What was that part? And besides that, my mama told me to always wear clean drawers—nothing about holey drawers. These are clean—they're just comfortably worn."

But before Betty could retort, she glimpsed a fast moving shape from the corner of her left eye.

Al was distracted in conversation. Halfway through the intersection, a speeding truck ran the red light and t-boned their car. It hit just behind the driver's seat. The back passenger's window-glass shattered as if a scoop-full of diamonds had been cast inside. It buckled the elder couple's car frame between the two side doors. Betty's head was whip lashed against her window. Al lost consciousness from the force of the blow. Their 1990's model Chevrolet was propelled sideways into a neighboring Taco Bell parking lot. The distracted teenager's SUV screeched to a halt off-center of the impact site.

Betty's ears rang. Although her sight was blurred, she could see her husband on a gurney near her. The sun was bright. She had no idea why she was outside on an ambulance stretcher. It took a moment to recognize the red and blue flashing lights. People in uniforms were huddled about them.

Slowly she regained her bearings and asked, "Sir, is my husband alright?"

The paramedic finished adjusting her

transport straps before answering Betty's question. "Ma'am, your husband should be fine. But he most likely has a fractured hip. We're gonna take y'all to the hospital now to check everything out."

Al was draped with a dark blue blanket. He had an oxygen mask over his face and was secured in a head brace. Betty noticed his tattered pants lying on the ground.

"Are those my husband's pants over there?" Betty inquired wearily.

"Yes, ma'am. We had to cut those off."

"Well, at least he had on *clean drawers*," she quipped.

"Well, we had to cut those off too, ma'am," the young man responded.

Due to the ringing in her ears, and the stress from the impact, it took Betty a moment to fully realize what she had just been told. Then she smiled and thought to herself, *Well, he's gonna get some new undies now, dad-burn-it.*

LEE ROY

He was one of God's gentlest creatures, but real scary looking when you first met him. His face was a mix of beet red and sun tanned grimace. Hair was shaved up the sides of his head with an unkempt flat-top. He squinted his eyes when outside. The only shape to his body was like that of a lumpy strongman, and he swayed from side to side like a willow when he walked. Mama said that she really didn't like the word *retarded* and we should just say he was *simple* or *slow*.

Everyone in town knew him. He would wave to us all and we all would wave and shouted back, "*Hey Lee Roy*." He even had his own seat at the show. Mr. Henny had a little brass tag made with his name on it. No one who knew anything ever sat in it. If you did, and he came in for the picture, there would be a ruckus. Nobody ever didn't get up from his seat. We called it the fat lady seat but Mama said it really was the love seat. We didn't know what that meant but we liked our name better.

After his Mama died, he went to live in the nursing home. Folks said she was an old lady when she had him. Lee Roy, they say, was as old as my Daddy. But he didn't look it. He kind of looked like he was just a big old baby man.

He liked to sit out front in his rocking chair at the Greyhound bus station. The gentle giant just sat rocking all day until a bus came in. Then he would help Mr. Saul unload the packages and take them out for delivery. Lee Roy was usually the first person the bus people would meet when they came to our town. He would say *Hey* to every one of them as they made their way down the steps of the traveling van. Lee Roy was known as the unofficial ambassador of our little, East Texas town.

It was also Lee Roy's job to clean the restrooms at the station. But he would only use the one marked with the COLORED sign. He did that regularly on account he loved to drink NuGrape cold drink as often as Mr. Saul would let him; and sometimes, even when Mr. Saul wasn't looking. In fact, it got to a point that Mr. Saul had to put the NuGrape in a special cooler. If you wanted one, you had to ask for it—or at least that is what the notice on the ice box said.

Mr. Saul often got onto Lee Roy about using the restroom for the colored folks. But the boyish man insisted he was to use that particular bathroom because he liked to color, as the sign indicated. Lee Roy once showed my brother and me a few crayons with a small book he had stashed in there as well. Mr. Saul had long been given dirty looks from some of the town's finer ladies because of this irregular practice by a slow-witted, white man. They told Mr. Saul it was not proper. He told them it wasn't any of their business and if they wanted their packages brought to their homes, they would just have to hush. So they did.

Lee Roy's excessive consumption of

NuGrape soda water may have contributed to what happened one warm, fall day. He had been especially busy delivering packages. After a long day of teaching at the elementary school, Miss Ellie Jenkins came home to find Lee Roy's hand cart inside her picket gate. It was at the end of her sidewalk which led up to the house. There was no sign of Lee Roy, but her front door was ajar. She thought perhaps the man had gone inside to put an expected package on the table since she hadn't been home.

When she got inside she called out, but no one answered. No packages were in the foyer. As Miss Ellie ventured farther back into the house, she noticed that the bathroom door had been closed. As any elementary teacher would do, she lightly knocked on the door but there was no response. So she opened the door, and there was Lee Roy with his pants down around his ankles, sitting on the toilet, and trying to manage a wipe. When he looked up at her, and she at him, Lee Roy let out such a loud, girly scream that a passing group of high school boys and their band teacher, Mr.

Abernathy, came running up from the sidewalk. They burst into the foyer where they met a shaken Miss Ellie. Not more than a moment later, Lee Roy came out crying.

"Miss Ella! I brought you package. I hada use ya' baf'room."

Tears streamed down the innocent man's face as Miss Ellie consoled him. It had been a fright to the both of them. Neither would have ever imagined the other in such a circumstance. The teacher had many times assisted younger children in such a position, but never a man of his age. However, she quickly assessed that although Lee Roy was much older than her, his mind was no more mature than that of one of her own students.

Miss Ellie assured the boys that everything was OK. She gave them an abbreviated account of what had just happened, and when Mr. Abernathy was satisfied she was not being molested in any egregious way, they left. Once Miss Ellie had gotten Lee Roy calmed down, as was her gentle way to do with children, she then offered Lee Roy some of her famous Presbyterian Chess pie and coffee. Lee

Roy accepted the pie, but refused the coffee.

Now this incident may have been the reason that Lee Roy never again left a package at anyone's home. If the recipient was not there regardless of if the door was unlocked, as most folks did in 1965, Lee Roy brought the parcel back to the bus station.

Mr. Saul certainly knew about the infringement of Miss Ellie. Any number of town's folk had told the story many times over and had retold it in as many ways possible as gossip can brew. The fact was that Mr. Saul was very instructional on Lee Roy's manners. The new rule of no leaving packages inside or out, due to the incident with Miss Ellie, made an impression on Lee Roy to do exactly what he was told.

A few months later, my mother was anxious to receive her package from the Montgomery Ward's catalogue. It was an oversized parcel that would be shipped on the bus. Because she was walking to town, she decided to meet my brother and me at school to help bring it home. My little sister was in her tow.

When we got to the bus station, Mr. Saul informed her that indeed the package had arrived. The only problem was that he had expected her to be home and that Lee Roy had taken it out for delivery. Mama was concerned that she must have missed Lee Roy on her way up. She explained that she did not know if her altered route to the school, or a stop at the library's bathroom for my little sister to pee had made her miss the delivery man. Never-the-less, Mr. Saul told her to just tell Lee Roy it was OK to give her the package if she saw him.

Since we were in town already, we asked Mama if we could go to the Square. My brother and I wanted to get some hot roasted peanuts at the Duke and Ayers candy counter. Mama said she really needed that package and didn't want to miss Lee Roy again. She needed us to help her carry it, so she got us NuGrape and Big Red soda waters from Mr. Saul's to appease us. We had to share with our sister as we headed home.

We were almost to the house when we saw Lee Roy. He had a big, brown package on his hand cart. When he saw us, he started squeezing the red, rubber, bulb on his bicycle horn. It made a loud, screeching, honk sound like my grandmother's geese. He met us happily singing his trademark song. The only one we had ever heard him sing.

"na na naaaaAAA…na na naaaaAA," was the simple, monotone chorus he echoed from his thick-tongued mouth.

Mama was thrilled to see Lee Roy—at first.

"Miss Peg, you got a package. It's nice to get a package."

"I know, Lee Roy. It's nice to get a package. Mr. Saul said you can give it to me now."

"Oh, no Miss Peg. You not home! You hav' ta' be home!"

"Yes that's right, Lee Roy. But Mr. Saul said you could give it to me now when I saw you."

My mother tried everyway she could to convince Lee Roy it was OK to give her that package, but he refused. He would not give her the package because she was *not home*. In the end, Lee Roy took the package back to the bus station singing happily on his way. Weary with three irreverent and entertained children, my mother marched us on home.

The next day, Lee Roy delivered the package. Mama tried to give him a quarter but he said, "Oh No, I can't take that—it's my job." But when she insisted he take the money for a cup of coffee at the Royal Café, he said he didn't like their coffee. He only liked Mr. Saul's coffee. My Mama had once told us that she never would drink Mr. Saul's coffee because it *just sits on the hot plate and boils all day*. She signed his paper and took the package inside. My brother and I walked Lee Roy down to the end of our street before saying goodbye to our friend.

May came before we knew it. Everyone was looking forward to the nearing summer break—especially our teachers. But what happened that month in our town, in the year of 1965, would never be forgotten. Lies would be told and lives would be changed. And Lee Roy would be at the center of it all.

High school was a restless time for kids.

Not quite adult, but still children in fact. So it was with the Baptist preacher's daughter. Next year, Becky would be in the twelfth grade. So would her boyfriend Tommy. They only had one more year to go. But as with many students suffering through the term's end, the swimming holes looked mighty inviting on warming days.

Lee Roy was delivering packages as usual. He sang his simple song and waved to the folks he met on his route. Many called Lee Roy *a retard,* but most were envious of his sense of direction and his extraordinary ability to find and remember addresses. The simple minded man was as much a cherished fixture in the town as was the Sam Houston statue at the court house on the Square.

The larger homes in the more affluent neighborhood of the municipality housed a few bankers, some doctors and the First Baptist Church's preacher's home. The Presbyterian preacher always joked with his followers that the Baptists always did everything in a big way. They had the biggest church in town, the biggest pastor's house, and the largest revival barbeques in the summer. The preacher said that they must need all of that to let God know they were the most pious people in the county—mirroring what heaven was like. Other church going folks in the community questioned that if that were so, *why did they have three Baptist churches in town*? That count didn't even include the one Negro church of the same denomination. *More like what they do in the biggest way is scandal and infighting*, deacons would say.

The alley way that Lee Roy often took for a shortcut to one of the banker's homes was shaded with large pecan trees. He enjoyed picking up the nuts and cracking them with his teeth to get at the flavorful meat. But on this day, the grass and gravel path was littered with broken, leafy, sticks. They had been knocked down by wind from a recent rain shower. The debris impeded his loaded down, two wheeled, cart. As he passed by a large brick home, he was arrested by the fallen refuse. Lee Roy had to adjust his wheels to get them unstuck from the small limbs. It was then he heard what he thought was a young woman moaning and crying out.

Lee Roy saw an open window at the back of the home. He heard the girl's cry again. The stout man left his cart full of packages and charged the window. He knocked in the screen and pulled himself through the opening. A girl lay naked on the bed. A man was on top of her and holding her hands above her head. The perpetrator's pants were off, but his unbuttoned shirt was on—he pounded her with his hips. Her face seemed to be grimacing in pain.

"G'olf her!" Lee Roy shouted. His massive right forearm side swiped the young man with a loud thud. The force was so hard that it tumbled the boy off of the bed and onto the floor.

The couple was momentarily stunned at what had just happened. Neither of them had heard the crash of the window screen.

"Lee Roy!" the girl screamed. "What are you dooooing here?"

"That man hurt'in you, Miss Becka."

The girl stood naked and shouting before Lee Roy. It confused him. The simple man averted his eyes from the girl as if he were ashamed to see her nude body. The boy scrambled for his pants. Becky hit Lee Roy repeatedly with her fists as he cowered, protecting his face. Finally, she reached for her blouse and partially covered herself. Lee Roy had heard nothing the girl had said about the boy being her boyfriend—nor would he have understood if he had.

"Becky! Becky!" another female voice cried out from within the house.

The young couple looked at each other but in terror this time.

"My mom! Go—get outta here. I'll take care of this!" she franticly whispered to the boy. And he grabbed his shoes and dove from the window onto the moist, leafy, ground.

"Becky! Becky!" the woman shouted as she burst through the door. Then the finely dressed woman screamed.

She saw Lee Roy standing opposite her. His shirt was disheveled as if someone had tried to rip it from his body—or get away from him. A lamp table was knocked over. The window screen was lying inside of the room, bent in half, and in the corner. The bed sheets were tossed about. The blue bottom sheet had an obvious, dark, wet spot on it. Her daughter was red-faced, sweaty, and her thin, white blouse only covered not too far from the bottom of her navel. She was pantyless.

Becky's mother grabbed the girl's arm and snatched her daughter from the room. She slammed the door shut, threw a chair in front of it, and dialed the operator asking them to send the sheriff.

When the law officers arrived, they found Lee Roy sitting on the edge of the girl's bed sobbing. He appeared to be afraid and disoriented. When another police car arrived, they led Lee Roy out in hand cuffs and took him to the jail at the court house on the Square.

"You'd expect this sort of behavior from the nig'rahs," Becky's mother commented about the simple man. "I'd never have thought a retard could do such a thing."

Once Lee Roy had been driven away, the sheriff, himself a deacon in the Baptist preacher's congregation, started the interview process with the girl and her mother.

It was revealed that it was her mother who had *saved* the girl. The woman had returned home after a Women's Circle meeting at the church. It was their annual spring luncheon for all of the ladies groups, and she had forgotten the Lemon Dill Mayonnaise sauce for her Tomato Salad Aspic. Her intentions were to grab the sauce and continue to present her dish at the event. As the preacher's wife, she was also expected to head the program of appreciation and installation of new leaders. It would have only taken her a few moments to run home and retrieve the overlooked condiment. *Thank God that she had forgotten it, lest her daughter could even have been murdered once the simpleton was finished having his way with her*, she surmised.

But the girl's account of what had happened was the most critical to the case. And the first thing the sheriff wanted to know was why she was not in school.

"I came home from class early because I was feeling ill," she started. "I had real bad cramps."

"It's her ladies time," the mother interjected as the sheriff gave a puzzled look upon hearing the girl's statement.

"Well, I was lying down on my bed. I was asleep. Nobody was home—I guess Mama went to the church. And the next thing I know is…Lee Roy was up on me! He ripped my panties off and I started trying to hit him! I rolled off of the bed and that's when he grabbed me again. He threw me to the floor and…oh, Mama!"

Becky began to sob loudly. Tears flowed from her eyes but they did not turn red, or puffy.

Becky's mother consoled her daughter in her arms. She asked the sheriff to give them a moment. The girl was now wrapped in a shawl and wearing a skirt to cover her hips and thighs.

A few moments later the sheriff asked, "Miss Becky. Did he…force himself inside of you?" He looked the discerning girl in the eyes. "Did he put his…?"

Becky squealed again with a high pitched moan and turned back into her mother's breast.

"Ma'am, I have to ask her. There's a wet spot on the sheets."

"I know, Sheriff," the mother replied.

Becky turned with a belligerent face and

said to him, "No! He did not!" The thought of Lee Roy in her that way disgusted her. But then another thought raced through her mind like a lighting bolt. She had caught herself in her own lie. "Well...I mean—I think it's my period. Or..."

The girl's mind raced faster as to what she should say. *What if I become pregnant? I told him to pull out before...blood—they can check to see if it's blood.*

"Oh I don't know! I don't remember!" Becky shrilled again, but this time her tears were real.

The sheriff finished writing his notes on a small leather bound note pad. He replaced it in his khaki shirt pocket. He then allowed the girl and her mother to leave the scene and they retired to the parent's bedroom.

As the sheriff was entering the living room from the back of the house, the pastor entered the home. He had been called and given a message to come right away, but the secretary had delayed the message while he was in a counseling session with a congregational couple. The concerned father first consoled his daughter and wife as the sheriff waited.

"Sheriff, how could this happen? What evil is this? In our town! In this little neighborhood. In MY house!" the pastor exclaimed.

The lawman went on to comfort the preacher as best he could and assure him they had everything under control. Before leaving, the sheriff said, "You probably should get your daughter to the doctor and have her checked out. I didn't see any signs of blood on her legs or on the bed. She said she couldn't remember all that happened. But it looks like it wasn't her period that stained the sheets. And if she was a virgin…"

"She is!" the pastor retorted. "She…well…she hadn't."

"It's Ok Pastor. We'll check Lee Roy out, too. He won't be going anywhere for some time. I'm just saying that…you may want to prepare yourself for anything unknown. Make sure she isn't hurt in anyway."

The two men parted with a condolence and an assurance that the lawman would be in church on Sunday. The drive back to the jail weighed heavy on the sheriff's mind.

"That damn retard peed his pants in the back of my car. Can you believe that?" one of the deputies complained. When I get that job in Huntsville, I won't be cleaning up crap like this anymore."

"Well it won't be the first time somebody did that. How many drunks have you hauled in here?" the jailer said.

Both men chuckled at that as they observed Lee Roy sitting naked on a cell bunk's, bare mattress. He was rocking back and forth, crying and singing to himself, "na na naaaaAAA...na na naaaaAA."

The prisoner had been in the jail for more than three hours before the interrogators had finally called Mr. Saul for help. No one at the nursing home in which the accused man lived, was available to come and check on him. Lee Roy had no other family, and the bus station proprietor was the closest thing to a guardian that he had—other than the state.

Mr. Saul and his wife had been neighbors with Lee Roy. The boy's parents had him at a late age—in their mid-fifties. He was their first and only child. At the time, it was considered a miracle that the childless couple had conceived.

The much younger neighbors, the Sauls, were trying to start a family of their own when he was born. Not long after his birth, Lee Roy's father died of a heart attack. That left his mother with a mentally challenged son and no income to support them. When Lee Roy's mother found a job at the Duke and Ayer's lunch counter as a cook, Mr. Saul's wife offered to baby-sit and look after the young man.

The Saul's raised Lee Roy nearly as one of their own, even giving him a job at the Saul's family owned business. But when Lee Roy's mother died, the young man was made a ward of the state. Mrs. Saul was in ill health after the birth of their fifth child. She was in no condition to take care of the grown young man. The Saul's made a deal with the state to have Lee Roy housed in a local nursing home and they would look after him as semi-guardians. When Mrs. Saul died, the widower continued to watch over the aging Lee Roy's affairs.

"Lee Roy! What have you done son?"

Mr. Saul exclaimed upon entering his cell.

"That boy hurtin' Miss Becka, Poppy. I make him stop."

"What boy? There wasn't anybody else there. Did you climb through that window into Miss Becky's bedroom, Lee Roy?"

"Yes, Poppy. He hurtin' Miss Becka. I stop him. I climb through da' win'da and knock him down. Miss Becka hit me and say, leave boy."

Mr. Saul sat with Lee Roy for the next half hour trying to make sense of what was happening. The simple minded man kept repeating something incoherent about another boy, but Lee Roy continued to sob and sing his song. He kept telling his guardian that he wanted to *go home*. But the father figure knew that he could do little more. And Lee Roy was left to the confines of his new residence.

It was not an easy thing for Lee Roy in the jail house. Although over the first few days several church ladies brought cakes and sweets for him, the abundance was eaten mostly by the sheriff's department. Intentions were good, but there was simply too much attention being placed on empathy for the jailed man, some thought. The counter protest of another group of church goers, mostly from the girl's father's congregation, petitioned that the sympathy be stopped. The sheriff finally relented to the protesters that demanded justice for the girl. The kindness had been allowed to continue for a month or so. But the final straw had been a visit to the Mayor's office from Becky's father.

Abuse also plagued Lee Roy shortly after the good will ceased. The deputy who had hopes of securing a job at the prison in Huntsville often hurt the man. Once the deputy had been accepted for the guard position at the prison, he was reassigned to the night jailer's position at the court house lock up. His replacement was given his patrolman's route for training. Three weeks remained before his new job started. Those were to be Lee Roy's most frightful nights.

The sadistic deputy hated Lee Roy. He could not tolerate his *crying and whining all the time.* The deputy often slapped Lee Roy. He would call him near to the door and prod him like a dog in a cage. The man cursed and spit on

154

the interned man. The lawman was careful not to leave a visible mark. There were no other witnesses to the man's crimes and Lee Roy was sworn to secrecy from his abuser by fear of retaliation and further harm. Even Mr. Saul had not a clue of the abuse.

One evening, the deputy was especially irritated with Lee Roy. The hour was late and the night dark. Lee Roy was sleeping when the man rattled his night stick loudly between the steel bars.

"Boo'yee…you smell like a dirty ol' dog. You shit ya'self?"

"No Boss," Lee Roy answered upon waking from the racket.

"Get up over here, boy," the deputy demanded.

Lee Roy feared he should do as he was ordered. He threw back his blanket. A few crayons that Mr. Saul had brought him fell to the floor when he disturbed his pillow. It was Lee Roy's habit to keep his colors and coloring book underneath his pillow when he slept. He picked them up and replaced them before standing up to meet the man in the fresh pressed uniform.

"Take off them clothes, boy. You gonna take a shower."

"I'm hada sh'er yester'dee, Boss."

The jailer rebuked Lee Roy and ordered him to do as told. Once the man was naked, he ordered the large man to put his hands through the door slot so he could handcuff him. Only then was Lee Roy led to the shower room.

The deputy verbally insulted the man on his way to the designated space. Once there, the lawman turned on the hot water—only the hot water.

"Boy, git up on in there," he demanded as he prodded Lee Roy in his bare back with his night stick.

Lee Roy was not the most intuitive of men, but he did know that judging from the steam bellowing from the shower head that it was hot.

"That hot, Boss!"

"Git yo' ass up on in there, retard!" The deputy swung and hit Lee Roy across the buttocks with his stick, registering a loud crack.

Lee Roy whelped and jumped into the

burning water. He cried out again in further anguish. The jailer saw that the water was much hotter than he had anticipated. It was leaving a dark, red, burn on the man's back. Lee Roy huddled close to the wall in order to relieve himself from as much of the spray as possible.

The deputy then reached in and pulled Lee Roy out of the way and turned the hot water faucet off, burning his own hand. He then put the cold water on full blast and ordered the prisoner back in. It was no more comfortable but it did soothe the man's blistered skin.

"Turn aroun' an' put your hands up against the top of that wall, Lee Roy," the jailer ordered.

"I can' reech tha' high, Boss," Lee Roy protested.

"Jus' do it! And spread your legs wide."

Lee Roy faced the wall and reached as high as he could against the small, white tiles.

"So you like ta' have your way with little girls, a' booyee?"

"No Boss. I ain' done nuttin' ta'…"

But before Lee Roy could answer, the deputy had cracked his night stick against Lee

Roy's bare bottom once more. The man screamed but the cool water did little to improve the pain as it flowed over the stricken flesh.

"You lie, boy! You a dirty beast! And I show you what we do ta' dogs like you!"

For the next ten minutes, the sheriff's deputy thumped Lee Roy's scrotum repeatedly between his legs with his night stick. When the prisoner would yell from the pain imposed on his testicles and try to close his legs, the jailer would again strike his buttocks and order him to spread his legs once more. When he tired of that, he ordered Lee Roy to bend forward beneath the water. The deputy began to forcibly prod at Lee Roy's rectum with the wet, wooden stick—all the time insulting him with questions of, *how does that feel?* And, *you want to know what it feels like to be a little girl don't cha'?*

The whole incident lasted no more than about fifteen minutes before the sadist tired of his game. Even so, the numbing cool water did little to console Lee Roy's offended body. Eventually, he was returned soaking wet to his cell. The feeble minded man fell asleep, softly sobbing and singing his simple song into the early morning hours.

It was the end of July when Becky and her best friend Debbie from church visited the pool.

"I don't know why those nig'rahs keep comin' over here and hangin' on the fence watchin' us swim. Don't they have a pond or somethin'?" Debbie remarked.

"I don't know and I don't care. As long as they don't mix with us, I'm fine with it," Becky answered while rubbing baby oil on her tanned skin under the high placed sun.

"Well, I do care. And I think your daddy would care too. He's says the bible says that the races shouldn't mix. Just like with retards." Debbie realized what she had just said to her friend. "Ooh. I mean...a..."

"Don't worry about it. I know what you mean. I hear my daddy preaching every day. You don't have to tell me anything."

Becky closed up the bottle of baby oil and straightened her towel.

"Debbie. There's something I wanted to ask you. My folks want me to have a pregnancy test done now to make sure that I'm…well, to make sure that nothing happened. After."

"Oh. Well didn't you go to the doctor after all that happened?" Debbie inquired.

"Yes. They did an exam. They didn't find anything," Becky responded stoically.

"Well…what about you and Tommy? I mean…the doctor didn't—what about your hymen?"

"I think that's an old wive's tale. Besides, I douched before I went. I told them I couldn't stand the thought of his seed being inside of me. It washed everything out. So there wouldn't have been any blood or anything. The doctor just told my mom that I was bruised inside real good. Besides, I've had my period since then."

"Oh. That's good," Debbie agreed.

"Yeah, Debbie but I need your help. I have to go to the doc again and this time they want a pee sample for the pregnancy test. I've been trying to get them to put it off as long as I could. It's been really making me nervous."

"So why is that? You've had your period. You can't be pregnant. Can you?"

"Oh Debbie," Becky cried as tears welled up in her eyes, "I don't think so. I mean I just don't know. But I need you to pee in a bottle for me so I can take it for the sample."

"What?" Debbie exclaimed.

"Well, I know it's odd, but I just couldn't live if I knew I was pregnant by that retard! I really need your help and you *are* my best friend from church." Becky did her best to sound desperately convincing.

"Well, I don't know. What if you are pregnant? I mean, I'm not saying you are. NO. I'm not saying…Well, haven't you gained a little weight lately?"

"Debbie!" Becky genuinely shouted, shocked at her friend's rude remark.

"No! I mean…I'm not…oh, Becky. I'm sorry. I'm just a little confused. I mean, Ok. I'll do it. I'll do it for you. I guess I'm just worried for you."

"Don't worry Debbie. I'm Ok. And if it makes you feel better, I will get checked out if something does go wrong. I mean, I have had my ladies time this month already. Tommy didn't like it when I turned him down last week," she chuckled, "but he got over it."

The girls carried on with their day in the sun and before leaving, Becky had her sample.

It was a good day for Lee Roy when his tormenter finally left for his new job. But on the jailer's last night, he had managed to insult the prisoner with one last rap of the man's knuckles. It hurt Lee Roy so bad that for days he was unable to color in his books. His hands even had to be bandaged. The deputy had explained it away as that Lee Roy had gone crazy and started beating the walls with his fists early in the morning because he wanted to *go home*.

Mr. Saul was meeting with Lee Roy in his cell several days later, when Aubrey McConnell arrived. The young defense lawyer had been appointed by the court to represent the accused.

"Hello, Mr. Harland Saul," the polite young man announced at the cell door.

"Hello, Aubrey McConnell. I hear you have another new daughter. Doesn't that make two?" Mr. Saul inquired as he looked up from reading his current issue of TIME magazine.

The young man chuckled. "Why yes sir, it does. Guess we're on a roll."

"Hey mis'a McConnell. Won' soma my grape drank?" Lee Roy offered.

"No thank you, Lee Roy. I've had one already today," the man replied with a neighborly fib.

It was Mr. Saul's habit to bring Lee Roy a bottle of NuGrape on his regular visits. He never forgot to bring it for his adopted son.

"Well, Mr. Harland, the sheriff is gonna let us have a room to talk about Lee Roy's case today. I hope we can get a case prepared for him and move this on along quick enough."

Moments later, after a bit of small talk at the steel bars, a newly hired jailer came to escort the three men to the reserved room. The deputy was much kinder to Lee Roy, but still his fear of the uniformed men had been impressed upon him deeply.

"Now Mr. Saul, there is something I just don't understand about this case at all," the lawyer started. "Lee Roy knew the alleged victim well. Didn't she help out at the home where Lee Roy has a room? As a candy striper?"

"Oh, yes. She has been a volunteer there for the past two years. Since she was a sophomore in high school. She will be a senior this year."

"Well, has there ever been any problem reported between the two of them? Or with any other females that you know of?" Mr. McConnell inquired.

"Never that I know of. The nursing home madam, Mrs. Peterson, does not allow any sort of shenanigans over there. She runs a tight ship. A no nonsense lady. I've had to move all of Lee Roy's things out of there. She will not put up with any foolishness perceived or otherwise."

The young attorney was taking notes as Mr. Saul continued his remarks.

"I don't understand it. The girl's family knows Lee Roy and myself very well. He has been delivering packages to the preacher's home and office for years. He even once carried their older boy to the church. He was about fourteen when he had a grand mal seizure and fell off of his bike in the middle of the road. Lee Roy saw him fall and went over to him. He was chewing up his tongue pretty bad. Lee Roy saw the blood and what was happening and stuck his fingers in his mouth. I don't know why he did that. Some kind of instinct I guess. Anyway, Lee Roy picked the boy up and took him to his daddy at the church. Left his packages at the side of the road. I remember it tore Lee Roy's fingers up pretty bad."

The scribe stopped taking notes and looked at the storyteller. Both men stared at each other for a moment. It was a curious thing that had been told.

"Well, did Lee Roy go to the hospital? And the boy?" the attorney asked.

"Well, no—not right off anyway. The boy did, yeah, I guess. But Lee Roy went back and delivered his packages before he started back to the bus station and showed me what had happened. He knows he isn't supposed to get side tracked. But sometimes Lee Roy's innocent nature is confusing to us normal witted folks. He usually does what he is told to do to a fault. He just kept delivering packages. Got blood everywhere. One of the ladies he delivered to called me at the station and told me he was bleeding all over everywhere— including her packages. He refused her help when she offered. Said he *had to finish his job.* I tracked him down on his route and took him to the docs."

Both men looked at Lee Roy sitting at the table next to them trying to color with his bandaged, stubby, fingers injured from the latest bruising incident. The gentle giant with the red face looked up at them and smiled boyishly.

"This does not add up, Mr. Saul. I have gotten word from the District Attorney that they intend on bringing aggravated rape charges on him. And being that the girl is a minor, and that her father is a prominent figure in the community, they also have hinted at trying to get the death penalty. Half of the town wants blood revenge. The other half doesn't know what to think. Our only political friend seems to be the sheriff. He seems to just be doing his job, or staying neutral in it all at least. Maybe he can help me further with some of the details. I just have a strange feeling about this, sir."

Mr. Saul told Mr. McConnell about the

mysterious boy that Lee Roy had mentioned early on. But no witnesses had ever reported any such claim. In fact, the only witnesses were Becky, Lee Roy and Becky's mother. Although the thought intrigued the young lawyer as a clue that could break the case as to why Lee Roy may have attacked the girl, there was no evidence to support anything other than the idea that he was *a sexual pervert*.

By the time school started again in September, Lee Roy had been locked up for nearly four months. His days now were spent as an in house trustee of sorts. He was regulated to cleaning bathrooms and cells when the weekend drunks were released. The town didn't have much of a crime problem. Lee Roy was the most famous of all criminals in recent history. And Becky was becoming a celebrity of unwanted proportion herself, at school.

For the first few weeks, teachers and fellow students expressed their condolences to her for what had happened. Everyone in town now knew of the offense against her. And although she first relished the attention, it soon became mundane. Not only that, but her lie was growing—inside of her.

The pregnancy test taken in the summer had come back negative. That was thanks to her friend Debbie. But now, even Becky had trouble explaining why she could not dress out for P.E. At four months pregnant, Becky developed a small pot belly. She dismissed it as an eating disorder from the depression she had developed from the tragedy. The athletic coach had pity on her and dismissed her from activities when she became hysterical and cried in an award winning performance.

Nearing the end of five months and close to Thanksgiving, her baby was growing rapidly. It could no longer be dismissed as an eating disorder. Her boyfriend Tommy was very concerned. The couple had remained seeing each other, but not as often as before. Becky also had stopped having sex with him regularly soon after the beginning of school. Now was the time to tell him that she was pregnant with his child and that their lie must be revealed.

"You can't tell your folks you're pregnant with our baby!" Tommy demanded. "You gotta tell them the truth! That the pregnancy test must have been wrong and that it's Lee Roy's kid!"

"I can't do that. It's not his, it's yours. And you need to marry me and take care of us!"

"How am I gonna do that? If I don't go to college, they'll draft me and send me to Vietnam like those other degenerates. My folks have money, but they won't be able to buy my way outta that. You gotta stick to the script and tell them the truth. It's Lee Roy's. And let your daddy decide what to do about it. They'll probably just want you to give it up for adoption."

"Well maybe I don't want to do that," Becky said. "Maybe I want you to marry me."

"Oh, no. I ain't ready for no wife and kid," the girl's boyfriend repeated.

The conversation went no where. Becky had to decide what to do on her own. Her decision came a day after the Thanksgiving holiday, after hearing how thankful her father was for his family. Surely he would be benevolent and understanding of her situation. But still, she was afraid to reveal the truth. So she started with her mother.

"Mama, I have to tell you something. I'm pretty sure I'm pregnant."

The preacher's wife was aghast. "What? What are you talking about? From that boy Tommy? Your daddy will have him thrown into jail with that retard Lee Roy!"

This was not the way Becky had envisioned the conversation going. The thought of Tommy being put into a cell with Lee Roy frightened her. Besides, she wanted to keep her baby and her soon-to-be, suggested husband.

"Aaa. No Mama. I'm...its Lee Roy's. I've never been with anyone else...anyone! The pregnancy test must have been wrong. I think I'm pregnant. I thought I was just gaining weight!"

"Oh sweet Jesus! I thought this nightmare was over. I thought you were just depressed and eating a lot more. Oh my God," her mother exclaimed. "We have to tell your father."

"Yeah I know, Mom. But I also want to keep it."

The woman screamed so loud, the pastor raced to enter the girl's room with a curious look of concern on his face.

"Your daughter is pregnant—and it's that retard's baby," the woman screamed.

The man's face turned a shade of red so dark it was almost purple.

"How!" he demanded. "The tests were negative."

"I don't know, Daddy," Becky genuinely sobbed, "But I want to keep it!"

"The devil you will! That is an abomination!" the man yelled while pointing at her belly. "How could you even say such a thing? That's worse than having a…a…a nig'rah baby almost!"

The man was livid with anger and fear. He paced the floor as the two women cowered together not knowing what he might do. They both knew well of his ill temper.

"You'll not be keeping any retard baby. Call the doctor. We need to get this taken care of. See how to get her an abortion! There won't be any abomination in my home. I can't even imagine either of you thinking such a thing! And besides that, they are going to fry that son of a bitch at the death house. The D.A. is seeing to that. And I'll be a witness." The man stormed from the house, bible in hand, heading toward the church.

Becky was confused as to why her father had mentioned an abortion. She did not really understand the full consequences of that, but she inferred it would kill the child. She was in a dilemma of her own making. And when she told Tommy what had happened, he said that he agreed with her father. It was only then that she realized how alone in her deceit she really was.

The next month was full of trials for Becky and Lee Roy alike. The young girl had fought hard to thwart her father's efforts to schedule an abortion for her. Lee Roy had struggled to maintain a happy demeanor during Thanksgiving, and now the coming of the Christmas holiday—his favorite of all for the child minded fellow. Neither could understand the path that they had been pushed down. Yet both suffered in their own worlds of shame without the considered knowledge of each other's pain.

Within a few days of the New Year, 1966, Becky's father made an announcement.

He had found a Baptist unwed mother's home for his daughter to give birth at. They would also make the baby available for adoption. The home was in Lubbock. She was to leave before school started back again.

But Becky was weary of the instructions she had been commanded to obey for the past months. She was going to be a mother. And she felt she deserved more than what her mother had been dictated to become. After all, where was the compassion of the Christian household? Did Jesus not say to *cherish all of the little children*?

After much self examination, the emotionally maturing young woman announced to her parents, "This is not Lee Roy's baby. It is Tommy's. And Lee Roy did not rape me. Lee Roy thought Tommy was hurting me, and burst through the window to save me. Tommy fled when I told him to. And when Mama saw Lee Roy there, I told her he had taken advantage of me. But I lied. And I won't give up my baby, or kill it, or have Lee Roy die either."

By this time the preacher had heard enough. He looked his daughter in the eye and said, "Whore. Your name betrays you. Because you are no redemptive Rebekah of the God's word—wife of Isaac. You are simply a whore. As your name means, *to snare*! No one will believe you. And I do not either. I cast your evil ways from my home. "

The young woman's mother pleaded for her daughter. But her father refused to hear of anything his wife may have said. The woman took pity on Becky. And relieved to know that the child may be born healthy, she quickly devised a plan for her daughter's welfare.

The pastor's wife had been raised Methodist. She had met her future husband while visiting a Baptist church in Dallas with a high school friend. The then seminary student had a gift for preaching. And the girl was taken by the young man's sermon on this particular day that he had been assigned to deliver the message. So much in fact, that she approached the man after the service and they developed a relationship from there. Later, they were married.

Her sister still lived in Dallas. She also had remained a Methodist. Over the years, the pastor had declared his wife's people *backsliders*. And that they *were no better then any other unsaved heathens*. But Becky's mother had always kept in touch with her family regardless. Now, it was time to save her daughter from a lifetime of convicted pain.

The three women came up with a plan to keep the pregnant girl close by. They would tell her father that they intended on sending her to an unwed mother's home in Pilot Point, just north of Dallas. It would not be as far away from at least some family. And even though she had been exiled by her father, the mother would still be able to have an assurance that her child had someone to safely watch over her nearby.

The preacher cared not where she stayed, as long as she was remanded to a strict Christian institution for reform. He knew of Pilot Point and approved of its program. The pastor agreed to it saying, "They aren't Baptist, but at least she won't contaminate any more of our flock."

It was done then. And Becky was put on a bus to Dallas to be enrolled by her aunt in the newly agreed, wayward mother's home—but with one exception. Her father knew nothing of the secret plan for the girl to remain with her mother's sister. And she was to keep the child. The man cared nothing more for his daughter, and washed his ignorant hands of her and her plight.

The new year found Lee Roy in better sprits. Many of the guards and deputies had become fond of him. They even played games like checkers and simple card games together. Lee Roy continued to clean the cells, deputy's bathrooms and prisoner's showers within the confines of the jail space.

Lee Roy's appointed attorney, Mr. McConnell, updated Mr. Saul on the case regularly. It had been several weeks since any real news about a trial date, or that any new evidence had been suggested. But early in February, that all changed.

Mr. Saul was sitting in one of the rockers in front of his bus station drinking his famously stout coffee. His hired of hand, a Negro named Buster, was sweeping up the restrooms. Mr. Saul had hired the young man a month after Lee Roy had been imprisoned. But Buster was not the only change that had occurred in the early months of Lee Roy's incarceration.

That August, President Lyndon B. Johnson had signed the Voting Rights Act of 1965. As an educated man, Mr. Saul had the foresight to see what was coming next. He took it upon himself not only to have Buster be more visible in the front of his shop, but he also had the hired hand to quietly take down the COLORED sign over the designated restroom.

Mr. Saul was one of the town's early advocates in the support of civil rights. And he paid such a price for it that it affected his shipping business. Half of the town was angry that justice was taking so long in the affront to Miss Becky, and the other half thought an injustice had occurred in the jailing of a simpleton—they truly believed that the whole story had not been told. In any event, Mr. Saul may have been able to disregard societal whims by taking down a sign, but he could not allow his colored man to deliver packages to any white homes. Much of his business went to *more legitimate* carriers. Even if he did have a white delivery man, Mr. Saul was still tarred with the same brush as Lee Roy, by some, because of his affiliation with him.

"Hello, Mr. Harland Saul," Mr. McConnell said in his usual, customary greeting. He always used the person's first and last name in a greeting as if it were habit to remember both names.

"Mr. McConnell," the elder man nodded while seated. A warm hand extended from the large puff of cigar smoke stoked by the elder of the gentlemen.

"Are you not cold, sir?" the young man asked.

"Well, Buster's in there sweeping up and the sun's out. The ladies don't care for my cee'gars so I take a moment outside everyday. Have a seat fella."

The two men sat for a while as the lawyer explained to Mr. Saul that Lee Roy's case had finally been set for trial. It would be in May.

"The District Attorney has spoken to the parents and to Becky's old boyfriend Tommy. He thinks they have a good case against Lee Roy," the lawyer said.

"Why did they talk to the boy? I never really liked him. He was of those that yakked it up pretty good about the time Lee Roy was found in Miss Ellie's house in her bathroom. I got a lot of grief from that. I think that's why some folks believe all this nonsense."

"Yes sir. Well I think that the sheriff always had a question about what exactly happened too. He's been quietly butting heads with the D.A. to look more into it. You know the sheriff's mother was in the same home as Lee Roy. He saw him there all the time. I'm sure he thought better of him."

"Yes, I knew her. She died a couple years ago," Mr. Saul replied.

"Well. There's just one more witness he has to speak with. But he feels he has the case wrapped up anyway. Becky's statement is clear. She named Lee Roy as her attacker several times over in the months before she left for Pilot Point. I believe she's due to have that baby soon. He wants to wait to bring her in till afterwards so it won't cause any more stress on her or the family. We just have to wait and see if she has anything else to say. Other than that, they intend to ask the judge for the chair."

Mr. Saul grimaced. "I thought they had a moratorium of sorts on the death penalty? That Johnson boy was the last they did since July. They executed 5 last year. There's plenty more there now—don't know why they'd stop."

"You're right, Mr. Saul. But the D.A. is still gonna try. They can still get him on death row till the courts straighten it all out."

Weeks more went by and the weather began to warm. The Redbud trees were the first to bloom, then the Dogwoods followed close behind. It was not only a sign of spring, but a sign of renewed life. And the flowers started showering the countryside.

In town, trees became full with green leaves. The rains came and baptized the expanding buds of the long awaited season of revival. And one day in the middle of April, a car arrived at the back steps to the courthouse.

Two women stepped out. One was in her late forties and wore a solid blue, pleated, short sleeved dress with a conservative bodice and covered shoulders. The younger girl, about eighteen, wore a similar styled dress. But hers had a more youthful, open neckline and the fabric was white with a flower print of yellow, Black-eyed Susans. The girl also carried a small bundle wrapped in a light blue, crocheted, afghan.

"Hello. I'm Rebekah Ames, and this is my aunt. I'm here to see the District Attorney, please."

"Yes, Miss Becky. He is expecting you. Have a seat and I'll make arrangements for y'all," the secretary said.

The two women waited patiently as they had been told. The heavy wooden chairs felt as uncomfortable as the hard marble floors they were placed upon. Becky remembered the time that she had visited her friend at the Presbyterian Church. *These chairs are as hard as those old pews*, she thought. *No wonder they call those church people the frozen chosen.*

The second story windows seemed grayed and dirty from the recent rains. Muffled voices and men's, leather soled shoes could be heard from the open design of the stairwell. But it was not long before a tall and slender, dark haired man in his fifties wearing a blue,

Seersucker suit arrived to greet them. They were led into an office with comfortable leather chairs and a huge oak desk.

After the polite greetings had been established, the attorney began.

"Miss Rebekah. I've asked you to come today because I need to establish the case against your attacker, Lee Roy. We are set for trial on Monday, May second. We'll be asking for the death pen…"

"NO," the girl interrupted.

"Beg pardon?" the lawyer asked as he looked down his thick, black rimmed eyeglasses at her.

"No. You can't execute him…for something he didn't do. I lied."

The man rocked back in his great, brown, leather chair, removed his glasses and folded his hands in his lap as the furniture gave a mournful squeak.

"Miss Becky. I have witnesses, including your mother, that says that this is the truth. Why do you suppose I should change the course of my case now?"

"Because I have had time to reflect. I am

a mother myself now. I have been living under the fear of my father, my social status in life, and my place in the church—just like my mother. But I will not be a part to the lies being told to protect the reputation of those most fortunate, at the expense of those less so. I believe in grace. And I intend to redeem myself. Because the Christian in me knows that if you don't answer for your crimes here, you surely will when you meet your Maker."

Becky went on to explain what happened that day. She told how she had skipped school with Tommy that morning to go to the river and swim, but then it started to rain. So they decided to go to her house. She knew her mother would be at her circle event, and that her father would be busy too.

When Becky and Tommy were having sex, Lee Roy burst into the room and knocked Tommy off of her. He thought he was hurting her. Lee Roy and she were friends at the nursing home that she volunteered at, she explained. He watched out for her there, and around town. They knew each other well. Mr. Saul knew her too.

But when Becky's mother returned for her forgotten dish, she heard the girl screaming at Lee Roy. Becky instructed Tommy to jump out of the window and she would make up a story on Lee Roy. She didn't think through the consequences. And the lie grew bigger.

"That's all very fine, Miss Rebekah. And I don't know why you would want to protect a retard, but you got pregnant. And that means your boyfriend Tommy would be the father if Lee Roy isn't. But he says he's not. Why should I believe you over him?"

Becky's aunt looked sternly into the man's eyes. She had had enough of the *good 'ol boy's* attitude of women being a man's property. But before she could speak, Becky snapped for her.

"I'm tired of being told by old men and foolish young boys that I'm less of a person then you because I have a vagina!"

Her voice was loud and strong. It was so loud as a matter of fact, that the attorney's secretary peeked through his office door window to check on him. He quickly dismissed the woman's concerns with an off handed wave for her to go away.

"I am not my mother!" Becky continued. "I lied and I will stand for it. But you will not have my help in inflicting anymore pain on anyone else in this town in my name. If you put me on that stand, I WILL tell the truth."

The rebuked man squirmed in his oversized chair. He rubbed his chin as the mannerism gave away his fearful thoughts of an unsuccessful trial.

"Well…what about this baby? If it's a retard too…then we know its Lee Roy's," the desperate man barked.

He knew the embarrassment he would face with at least half of the town's people. There had been many who had questioned the entire circumstances of the event. Many had suspected that something out of the ordinary had happened. And when the girl's announcement of pregnancy came so much later, it made others believe it was all a hoax to cover up the truth about Lee Roy and Becky's relationship. Perhaps even that *she* may have been the perverted one.

"He's fine! Thank God. He has all of his

fingers and toes…and he even looks like his daddy," she finished softly.

Becky lifted the baby from her chest, turned him to the inquisitor, and pulled back the shawl. A bright eyed, three week old, baby boy with crystal blue eyes gurgled and sputtered once revealed. His hair was red and his cheeks chubby. The boy's fair skin was as pink as the petals on any one of Becky's mother's prized spring roses.

"You see, sir. His hair is red like his father's," the girl with the blonde locks started. "Both Tommy and I also have blue eyes. Lee Roy's are brown. And his skin is darker. His mother was Spanish they say. He always kept a picture of his parents next to his bed. I know because I volunteered at the nursing home he lives in. Lee Roy is not this baby's father."

Not much more could be said. The truth was obvious to everyone in the room. The only factor to be considered now was what to do with Lee Roy. But that would not be decided right then, the attorney interjected.

As Becky and her aunt reached the bottom of the stairs, they saw Mr. Saul entering from the front glass doors. Becky said to her aunt, "I have one last person to see before we leave this place for good."

"Hello Mr. Saul."

"Becky. Well, I...," Mr. Saul stumbled as his words were caught with surprise.

But the girl quieted his mind with her newfound, mature and motherly demeanor. And the three of them made their way to the basement within moments of their greeting. Mr. Saul was carrying two bottles of NuGrape soda water.

The jailers made a room ready for the group. Lee Roy had been cleaning the showers when they told him he had a visitor and that he needed to wash up a bit. He washed his hands and face in cold water. He had not used the hot water for showers or hand washing for several months. The guards thought this to be an oddity, but he simply refused anything but cold.

"Hey Miss Becka! How you?" Lee Roy exclaimed. He hadn't seen his friend in months, and he was very happy.

"I'm fine Lee Roy. And you?" she asked.

"I good Miss Becka. Got a new home! I

not home there anymore."

"I see that Lee Roy," Becky said feeling the tears well up in her eyes.

"Hey! Who dat Miss Becka? You got a baaa'beee? It's nice to have a baa'be."

"Yes Lee Roy. I have a new baby."

The young mother pulled back the shawl so Lee Roy could see his face. Lee Roy's eyes grew big and he giggled when the child blew bubbles from his tiny lips.

"He little, Miss Becka. He little and funny!"

"Yes he is Lee Roy. His name…"

"Can I touch him, Miss Becka?" the giant baby-man interrupted.

Mr. Saul looked uneasy. So did the girl's aunt. Instinctively they started to say something to Becky, but before they could she said, "Yes Lee Roy. You can touch him."

Mr. Saul almost knocked over the bottles of NuGrape sitting on the table as he tried to grab Lee Roy's arm. The aunt had a look of fear on her face as she steadied the drinks. But Becky gave a stern "Ssssshhh" to them both.

"Go ahead, Lee Roy. It's Ok."

Lee Roy reached out with his massive hand, curled his fist, and pointed out his index finger. He gently touched the child's tiny exposed hand. The baby grasped his finger and looked up at him.

"He like me, Miss Becka. He's a nice baa'be."

"Yes Lee Roy. He likes you."

Lee Roy smiled as the infant tugged as best he could with his feeble fingers at the man's own digit. "What his name, Miss Becka? He have a name?"

"Yes, Lee Roy. He has a name. Two names—like you. It's Lee Harland. Named after the two kindest men I know."

"That like me, Miss Becka! Two names." Lee Roy thought a moment. "Lee Harlan'. That a nice name. It's nice to have a nice name."

"Yes it is, Lee Roy. Yes it is," the girl confirmed.

The group sat and visited for several minutes. Mr. Saul offered Miss Becky his NuGrape and she and Lee Roy drank their cold drinks and admired the baby. They sat side by side as they often had in the past when she would read story books to him.

When the time had come for them to leave, Lee Roy asked if he could kiss the baby. This time Mr. Saul and her aunt had no reservations. And as Lee Roy leaned down to gently kiss the child on his forehead at his mother's breast, Becky in turn kissed the top of Lee Roy's flat-top and whispered, "I'm sorry."

Lee Roy straightened up and gently placed his open palm upon her cheek. He looked into her blue eyes as if he understood her apology.

The next week, it being the last week of April, Mr. Saul found himself sitting at a table in his bus station watching Lee Roy sweeping the floor.

"Mr. Saul, I done swept that flo' already today, suh."

"I know, Buster. But your job is still secure here. Don't worry about it."

"Ok. But when I was cleanin' up in that back bathroom outside, I found these crayons." The man of color set his gray, steel, pail down beside him. "And somebody done took yo' TIME magazine in there too. You said you had been missin' one. Maybe this a' it."

Buster leaned down and placed the colors on the table before Mr. Saul. He then gave the elder white man the journal with the crumpled cover.

Mr. Saul looked at it. *TIME The Weekly Magazine*, he read silently. *Is God Dead?*

Harland Saul looked over at Lee Roy as he swept the floor. He was singing to himself, "na na naaaaAAA…na na naaaaAA."

Lee Roy suddenly stopped. With one hand holding onto his broom, he used the opposite to pick up a bottle of NuGrape from a nearby counter. He took a swig, and then smiled at Mr. Saul.

Mr. Saul smiled back at Lee Roy with a cup of coffee of his own in hand. He picked up the copy of TIME, tossed it in the trash can next to him, and said, "Not today he's not. Not today."

ABOUT THE AUTHOR

Author KT Ashely is an American writer from the South whose genre is Historical and Realistic Fiction. He is a native of Louisiana but currently splits his residency between Georgia and Mississippi. Much of his writing is influenced by historical events from contemporary to ancient. The human condition and it's affects on society are often the theme. Plot lines involving prejudices, indifference, wealth disparities, and military service are common.

KT recalls his first major writing piece in the fourth grade. Tilted *Scorpio*, the short story involved a human/arachnid mutant that rampaged through the city. It most likely was inspired by the Godzilla movies of which he was a huge fan. This intense interest in Science Fiction led him to read stories by H.G. Wells, Ray Bradbury and others. Later in life, he was inspired by Harper Lee, Ralph Ellison and George Orwell, plus his own exposure to life in rural America, travels abroad, and military service in the U.S. Naval Nuclear Submarine Force during the Cold War.

"I love the English language and the endless possibilities of structure and vocabulary. With the correct diction, one can create a beautiful piece of artwork that the reader is so satisfied with—he will want to read on and remember." —KT Ashely